YUMA'S SMILE

A novel by

RANINE

ISBN (Print): 978-1-54396-357-1
ISBN (eBook): 978-1-54396-358-8

To Yuma; all my love for you has been written in the lines of this book. All you have suffered and those like you who have suffered in similar ways will be heard. I love you more than anything this world can offer or will ever be able to express.

To Mr. Michael Field; for if it were not for you, the existence of this book would not have come into fruition. Thank you kindly and deeply, you will always be the best father any girl could adopt. Thank you for keeping me sane all these years.

To my best friend Penny, thank you for showing me what true loyalty and support means. You've always been and continue to be my family. I would not have enjoyed my life if you weren't a part of it.

To my supporters; thank you for staying with me along this journey. Your support and feedback have done well in aiding me through this process. I love you guys!

CONTENTS

PREFACE

The drive out of Syracuse took us fifteen minutes into an area where houses stood a significant distance apart. Turning onto a street, where you saw neighborhood watch signs posted on telephone poles and a school district in your backyard, you could hear the privilege before you saw it. It was nothing like living within the city, where the houses were on top of the other or the noise of city life interrupted your peace of mind at all hours of the night, along with the sound of the city bus stopping at every corner.

The air whooshed its way inside the car on this particularly sunny day, leaving little room for the humidity to tackle us down.

"We're almost there!" Yuma notified us with much excitement. I had to admit, I was beyond excited to see this good news she'd been keeping from us for so long. My body was practically shaking in glee. The buzzing of my phone caught my attention then; pulling it out, I skimmed the text and smiled before containing the blush on my face and responding. Not wanting to bring any attention to myself, I stuffed the phone back into my pocket and continued looking out the window.

Turning into a driveway, the engine cut off and Yuma turned to us: "Welcome to our new home!"

Ilham, Ayman, Nur and I all exchanged looks. There was no way we were going to live in a nice neighborhood with our own backyard and quiet neighbors! Filing out of the car behind Yuma, we ran into the empty house and examined each room with awe. The skylight in the dining room was, by far, my favorite--the way the sun poured in gave me a great feeling of hope. It was a new beginning--one Yuma deserved more than anyone.

Nur ran throughout the house chasing her echoes, while Ilham and Ayman asked Yuma loads of questions. Walking into the living room, where two giant windows faced out into the front yard, I stopped and admired the view. Maybe it was the way the house looked--completely empty, new, ready for a family to move in and start making memories--or the way the sun filtered through the glass; maybe it was how the entire room lit up golden and warm.

Something just felt different.

"So, what do you think Amani?" Yuma asked me as she stood beside me in sweet contemplation. I turned to her then, still stunned at how brave and strong of a woman she was, wanting so desperately to give her the world. I feel so lucky to have been raised by someone as courageous and undefeated as she.

"You've finally got the house you've been dreaming of Yuma; I'm so proud of you."

"No Amani, the house isn't what I dreamt of. Seeing my children happy in a loving home is what I've dreamt of. It's taken twenty-one years of suffering and heartbreak, but we're here together now. We can start anew, and this time, we can all build it together."

I hugged her then with my eyes tearing up. She felt small in my arms now, so frail yet, so strong. Kissing the side of her head, I let the tears fall as I pulled back to admire the sun enveloping her face. She stood there looking so regal, and so very proud. She had delivered herself despite her hardships.

She was finally in a place that she could call her own, and for that, I smiled.

PART ONE

CHAPTER 1

Beginnings

"In the end, it all begins."

– Saji Ijiyemi

You live your whole teenage career aiming for one event. Within that event lay countless moments which follow up the finale. That major event I speak of? High School Graduation.

The event that marks the beginning of young adulthood with brand new lessons and new experiences making up moments leading up to another life defining memory.

Well before we get to that moment I'd like to finish this one right here. Staring at my cap in hand, feeling the cloth above the cardboard made me feel pretty amazing. I was now the second in our family to successfully complete high school and walk the stage for my diploma.

Slipping on my robe and placing the cap firmly on my head I stared right back at my reflection and smiled, "today is the day!"

Moments make up the fabric within the events of our lives. Overtime that fabric becomes the quilt of our story to pass onto generations. I knew my quilt just had to be amazing right? Surely, she would be there smiling right?

She once said, "When I see you guys graduate high school I'll be happy."

"Amani Abdel Nour," Mr. Deflor, my principal called out rather incorrectly. I gripped the curtains for strength, knowing deep in my heart that she was not going to be smiling, but hoping all the same.

I put my best smile on and walked onto the stage, and while I knew I should have been watching the principal and my diploma, I couldn't. I was scanning the crowd for my mother's emotionless face. I saw Ilham in the front row, whistling. Nur and Ayman sat next to her. But Yuma was nowhere to be seen.

My heart dropped not seeing her beside them cheering. Why would she do this to me again? Why would she make yet another promise and fall through on that spoken agreement?

Tears flooded the seats within my water line, all of them bracing to show their support and come racing down my cheeks to comfort me. This was all a joke. As if things couldn't go any worse I nearly tripped on my robe almost causing me to kiss the surface of the stage.

Clearing my throat as if to rid myself of the embarrassment I felt, I continued on. Centering my attention to Mr. Deflor's hand who lay extended towards me in honor of my countless years of hard work, while successfully managing to lay below the radar, awaited my approval.

"Thank you," my voice cracked placing my own hand in his with a firm shake. Holding the diploma-less frame I quickly walked off the stage to meet my family.

Ilham embraced me first in her own sister like manner, "Congrats kid, you're going to be up in Cuse with me come fall!"

I gave a weak smile, "Yea."

Ayman was next as he jumped on top of me, "Both my sisters are leaving me now! Does that mean I can have your rooms?"

"No," simultaneously Ilham and I corrected. But I couldn't keep my emotions from showing to which Ilham picked up on.

"Yuma tried being here for as long as she could," she sighed.

"Yea well it wasn't long enough."

As soon as we were back at home I couldn't contain the anger I felt, we filed into the house while our dad demanded we powder our noses and get ready to dine out in celebration. But my focus was on one person.

"You stayed for the whole thing EXCEPT the most important part!" I yelled, "you were the one who wanted us to graduate and get an education! What's it worth if you aren't there to SEE it!"

"Amani," she sighed, "I get tired of sitting near a bunch of people, you know that."

"Tired? You get tired on the day of my graduation! Who says that to their daughter!"

She waved me off then. A conversation with Yuma was like talking to a wall; cold, hard and one sided. She stared at me as I spoke in excitement, action and adventure attached to every word. She looked at me and I saw the faraway look in her eyes. A look that told me no one was home. I wondered if anything I had said registered in that brain of hers.

She finally spoke. "When I see you guys graduate college I'll be happy."

I knew on the day I crossed the University's stage there would not be a smile. Her depression had dug itself deep into the smallest and deepest corners of her heart; it's disabled any ability for her to show and feel love.

"I go to school and I see everyone walking with their families speaking to one another and laughing. But our family isn't like that! Why? Why can't we enjoy being with one another? I just want to know that you care about what goes on in my head! Can't you just try once?" Tears ran their familiar path down the hills of my face. It was the same tune but a different day.

Yuma looked away from me then and responded with a voice that seemed to take every bit of energy away from her, "I don't love anyone Amani. I'm just waiting for my death to catch up to me."

I dropped my head, my hair cascading down my face like a curtain hiding my disappointment from her. Why did she have to say things like that? Why did she have to make it seem like living was her hell. My eyelids fell heavy and my arms lay limp by my side. There was no point in speaking to her. She would never listen or care, so why do I keep trying? Maybe it was because I hoped that if I spoke to her enough times or if I pressed her to talk to me, eventually she'd get the message.

Only time would tell and so far, it's been seven years since I last remember her happy. Her happiness came from hope, hope that with the release of my felon father our futures would become better. Sadly, with his release came her inevitable fall to rock bottom.

CHAPTER 2

Father

"When you have expectations, you're setting
yourself up for disappointment"

– Ryan Reynolds

S ummer in Upstate New York felt like a sauna, the air thick and
the humidity thicker. Days like this were long and dull, needing
to remain indoors so that you could jump in the shower to chase away
the stickiness of July. To an outsider, today would look as picturesque as
any other. A true getaway for families to swarm to for a nature walk out-
ing. The neighborhood was unusually quiet which was something that
rarely ever happened on the North side. Kids were always screaming as
they chased one another, parents sat on their stoops watching over their
children, and occasionally we would be graced by the infamous couple
always fighting about something you'd most likely see on trashy reality
show. Today seemed to be an off day for the pair which left Ilham and
I sweating on our porch just watching the trees slightly sway and the
wires above buzzing so loud it made the temperature rise a few degrees.

To think that a year ago I graduated high school and in one month I would be headed back to college. Time really flies, that terrified me.

"Do you ever think about what our lives are going to be like ten years from now?" I asked her playing with the tail end of my braid.

"Away from here that's for sure," she responded with a sigh, "but I can't leave Nur behind, if I can't take her with me I'm staying."

"I wonder what our lives would have been like if we had an actual family you know? Like if we really spent time with one another instead of hiding ourselves away."

Ilham watched the birds on the lawn pick apart some slices of bread we threw out for them earlier. She seemed deep in thought, biting her lip before responding, "That's not the life we grew up living though. No use in pondering over what isn't ours to control. Our lives aren't American, we grew up here but we don't get the same luxury." She looked off into the distance then, I could see she, like I, was not happy with the life we were given. "Arabs here don't know what family is or how to be one. I just want to do something crazy, just to see if all this stress is really as big as they make it out to be ya know?"

"Like dating?" I questioned eyebrow raised,

"Maybe" she entertained, "let's see if his threats about killing us are really legitimate."

"Whoa, that's risking a lot to test a hypothesis." She shrugged her shoulders continuing to stare out into the quiet street. Thoughts roaming her mind endlessly.

I knew she was talking about Alzalim in that moment, they never got along, always butting heads. She wanted him to be the dad we needed, and he never wanted to be a dad. Life is cruel that way, giving people children when they don't want any and making it impossible for those who do to even have the chance to birth one. We were good kids and yet he never took the time to see that, he or Yuma for that matter.

People would argue that my father was a good man. People, like his siblings, said that my mother chased him away. Chased? I don't think so. Annoyed? Possibly.

Many claimed to know "the story" because my father had told them the "truth." But his siblings, especially, should have known their brother well enough to know that: he was a con man, not to be trusted. Ever. When it came to their honour and dignity, however, they chose to accept his version of the facts to ward off any negative rumours and whispers being spoken of in their family name. In turn, they placed blame on my mother and her family name, causing her claims to sound ludicrous no matter how hard she fought against his false accusations.

Yes, people would argue that he was a great man...that my father was filled with stories and wisdom beyond his age. I truly believe that my gift for stitching words together came from him. Once you saw him in action, there was no denying that this man was one of the greatest story-tellers. But his words were used to mimic the truth. They were lies spun to benefit him, leaving those who heard him in awe and admiration.

I'd watch from afar and shake my head at his dirty tricks; he never did anything unless it benefitted him. He never gave a penny unless he expected a nickel in return. This man was the devil walking amongst us on this earth; he was pure evil and didn't care if people saw through his poorly constructed disguise, because by then, it would be too late.

In the span of just three years, this man brought so much heartache for my mother, so much change and destruction before leaving our home, that we were left with the impossible mission of rebuilding much of the destruction left behind. The aftermath made us question whether he'd had a heart to begin with or if he'd sold it to get his fix.

My siblings and I were filled with so much anger for him. Somehow, my baby brother and sister still carried and clung onto a small bit of hope within their hearts, believing that he still loved us. But I remain ashamed and disgusted to be related to such a vile man.

My aunts and uncles would say, "Think of all the good he has done for you, do not be so quick to judge just because it wasn't done in the way you saw it best. Mistakes of one man do not define him."

Of course, there was some truth to that, but when he persisted in making the same mistakes repeatedly (especially the ones that led him back into prison), they no longer qualified him to be forgiven.

He was sent away when I was five years old, my older sister Ilham was six and Ayman was three. Nur had not been born yet, for she came along eleven years after Ayman. Our entire childhood consisted of visiting him every weekend in prison with false promises and dry kisses. Our playground consisted of the wired fence they kept around the picnic benches and felons. There, we'd play tag with other inmates' children around arsonists, drug lords and other types of criminals I didn't understand much as a child. We were such frequent visitors at that prison that the guards knew us by name and greeted us every week, until I was convinced these routine visits were as normal as attending school.

All three of us would sit at the worn out wooden square table and stare up at our father who smiled as if he'd won the lottery. You'd swear it was genuine, but as I grew older and wiser I noticed he'd put on an act, in order to be guaranteed a visit, food and money in his account for God knows what they exchanged as currency. Jail was a lonely place for a guy like him. His con ways wouldn't fool other prisoners as easily as they fooled the outside world. These people were like him; they knew dirty business when they saw it, and my father was one of the worst con artists there.

My mother had so much life in her eyes then. She'd hold my father's hands so tight that blood rushed in to supply his fingers with life. Her smile is faint in my memories of that time; oh, how I wish I could remember it so. But as a child, items such as Swedish Fish catch your attention more than something as simple as a smile.

My father would sit in his chair with his beige apparel and look at all three of us: "When Baba (daddy) gets home we're all going to go to Disney World!!"

We'd stare at him with such admiration and joy because, as kids and even as adults, Disney World was something of a dream.

He'd turn to my brother then and kiss his forehead, "You and I are going to go fishing baba."

"Fishing?" Ayman asked in disgust, chewing off the head of the Swedish Fish.

My father kept his smile strong, "Yea, it's Baba's favorite hobby, I'll teach you okay? It'll just be me and you time."

With the promise of having quality time with his father, my brother smiled wider than you can imagine, his toothy grin with varying-sized teeth trying to find their place in his mouth, giving away his aging youth. It was like that with all of us during our visits at the prison. We'd compete for his attention because we had a limited amount of time to speak with him. Although my mother always won, given that we didn't have much to talk about with him, he didn't try to know us and we didn't think enough to care.

She hoped for his release. You could tell on our drives to the federal prison and coming home. She smiled then, awaiting the day my father would be set free and save us all from the brink of poverty. Her golden go-to line, "when your father gets home," seemed to be the response she gave us after every question we raised; so much so, we could do nothing but wait and hope along with her.

We'd receive many letters from my dad, filled with drawings and sketches of Disney characters saying the words in the letters he'd write us. The letters were so frequent one might believe he wrote one every day. He'd become a sort of business man while in prison, drawing portraits and making unique cards to sell to others in the stonewalls that became his home.

"A great man," they said.

In time I would see he was nothing short of the devil with his intense gaze and demonic smile. He was a curse sent to us, for I don't believe God would test our faith with such a horrible man. Not even his toughest warriors could withstand a man without a soul.

He would come to invade my headspace, wedge his way into my life when I didn't want him to, like a persistent ringing that would never leave.

Riiiing riiiing

Ilham and I both turned our heads to look inside the front door connected to the porch, I noticed the phone ringing and headed to the counter where Yuma's cell was buzzing with small vibrations on the granite countertop.

"Yuma your phone!" I yelled upstairs,

"Tayib (ok), answer it," she responded back.

Grabbing her phone, I noticed that she didn't have this number saved. Clicking "answer," I held the phone to my ear, "Hello?"

"You're receiving a collect call from..." the automated voice message informed me just as his voice cut in.

"Alzalim Abdel Nour." There it was, the voice that caused my body to panic. My heart begged to be released and run as fast as I could, away from any sign of him.

"Press one to accept or hang up to end the call," the automated voice continued.

Lowering the phone, I hovered over the "end call" button. I could end my anxiety over speaking to him right then and there. I could remove the burden of confronting my fears. I didn't like that I trembled so much in his presence; I didn't like that all my strength seemed to be sucked dry whenever he came around, or that my vocal cords became mute. I was like a lion lacking the courage needed to rule over the jungle. Taking a deep breath, I clicked "one" and slowly brought the phone to my ear.

Closing my eyes tight, I let out a small, "Hello."

"Amani?" he asked, feigning interest.

"Yea," I confirmed.

"How are you Baba?"

"I'm good."

"Yea, what you been up to?"

"School," my heart clawed its way up my throat, begging to escape. I swallowed hard, wanting this to end as soon as possible.

"Yea, what's been going on?"

I looked around me, the kitchen hadn't changed since I accepted the call, nor had the stillness of the street. Everything was as it was since before he called. I don't know why I expected the skies to crumble and the ground to break open, consuming me from the mere sound of his voice.

"Nothing, nothing ever goes on," I swallowed. I felt my body shaking now, I felt the fear as strongly as I have always felt it. I hated that; I hated how pathetic I was around him.

"Where's your mom?" He asked, wanting as desperately as me to end our not so exciting conversation.

"She's upstairs, hold on."

And so, I ran. I ran as fast as I could, as if the phone itself was hot coal that I desperately wanted to remove from my hands. Barging into Yuma's room, I climbed on her bed and deposited the phone onto her lap.

She looked at me with confusion, "Who is it?"

"Yaba," I responded shoving the phone away from me, glad to be rid of it. She rolled her eyes and sighed before picking up the phone.

"Hello," her voice reached out to him like a lighthouse, as if he swam lost at sea.

I pulled out of her bed and slowly walked out of her room. I know he's my father and all, but he sure as hell didn't feel like one to my heart or instincts. I trusted my gut more than I trusted him.

Something felt ominous; it just didn't feel right. There was nothing I could do but wait to find out. Time reveals all. At least, that's what they say. But I was more willing to keep time from ticking, in the present as it was now, rather than have him come home.

CHAPTER 3

Farah's Arrival

"Take care of your memories, for you cannot relive them"

– Bob Dylan

I t was a Saturday morning as I awoke to the sun's warm hand nudging me conscious. The summer seemed to drag on slowly, and that wasn't something I was quite fond of. Unlike many others, summer vacation this year was the absolute worst time for me, given that it usually meant I was home with my father and a family that hardly spoke to one another, let alone spent time with each other.

Summer meant no escape from the reality I was in; there was no distraction from the sadness waiting for me at home. I was distant and detached from my friends then. Engulfed by the dark abyss that consumed my home, I no longer had the energy to socialize. I had to conserve my energy to be able to defend my mother against my father alongside Ilham.

Luckily, he'd been gone this time, for a little over a year and our home was nothing short of peaceful, as a result. Everything good must come to an end eventually though. That was the day I feared.

I rubbed my eyes as a yawn escaped me. Staring at the ceiling I wondered if I was going to do the same thing I did every other day during the summer or if an opportunity would present itself to do something different.

Getting out of bed I continued onto my morning routine before heading down to grab some oatmeal for breakfast. My mother was already awake then, drinking her cup of coffee as she stared out the window looking drained. The smell of dark roast with sugar snared my senses, persuading me to make some of my own,

Why not, I thought. *It may just wake my soul up for once.*

Early mornings were always my favourite, when home from school. Don't get me wrong, I'm not a morning person but during the summer I easily became one, as a result of going to bed around nine or ten. I felt great waking up as early as seven or eight, getting to see the sun rise up as well--it was all a rare sight for me during the academic year at SU. Going to bed late and waking up even later was my college student routine, but that habit wouldn't take at home, I guess.

I leaned on the counter and looked into the empty street watching as the sun began its steep journey into the sky. A few birds chirped endlessly as they picked rice off the roof of our garage. Instead of throwing food out that was about to go bad, we'd throw it on top of the garage roof so that the birds, squirrels and cats would take their fair share.

Once my instant oatmeal was ready, I grabbed my cup of coffee and sat opposite of my mother. She was still staring out the window, dwelling on her thoughts, I assumed. We didn't speak, there was no point in speaking anyway because nothing ever happened, and Yuma (Mom) seemed to be absorbed in her own world. So, we usually just sat there in silence while we finished our breakfast and took in the calm summer mornings.

My heart ached; I was sad, extremely sad. Mentioning it out loud only made us aware of our own sorrow causing the air to thicken and our moods to plummet. I just sighed then, wanting to cry, but not being able to because it took too much effort. So, I just washed my dishes, put them away and grabbed one of the many books in my library to occupy my mind and trigger my imagination.

"I'm going to Khaltich's (your aunt's) house, you coming?" she asked just before I was able to head back up.

I enjoyed visiting my aunt, so I looked to her then, "Yea why not, there's nothing else to do."

She dropped her coffee mug into the sink then and began her trek upstairs. I followed her to get dressed myself, but stopped in front of Ayman's door and gave it a knock. With each passing year, we saw less and less of him. He was always locked in his room talking on the phone with one of his friends or another gamer. He hardly spoke to us, and as much as we tried, we could never get him to open up. He was a mystery to us all. I never knew what was going through that head of his or how his father's departure affected him.

"Who were we kidding," I thought, "even when he was around he was never around."

"Yea" a deep mumbling voice responded.

"Open the door" I ordered softly.

"What do you want? I'm in bed"

"Then get up and answer the door so I can tell you" I retorted annoyed.

Was it so hard to just open the damn door and speak to me face to face? I wondered. I hardly saw him anyways.

A rustling noise sounded before a groan was heard; his movements were slow and pained, due to a longboarding accident he had got into a while back, since then he'd been in consistent pain around his hips and below them. He'd been to numerous screenings since, but nothing could be found. I imagined him moving as if he was close to death, with the grim reaper watching his hourglass ticking sand away.

I felt bad for making him answer the door. I should have just let him be, but I really wanted him to spend time with us and as a family. God only knows when we'd ever get the chance to see him. The door unlocking caught my gaze; he opened it just enough to expose one eye.

"Yea?" he asked. His visible eye looked heavy with exhaustion.

"We're going to Farah's house, want to come?"

I knew he'd say no; he hadn't seen our aunt in a long time. What's sad is that she was the only sibling Yuma had in America. She also happened to be the only aunt who gave a damn about us. Everyone on Yaba's (Dad's) side always had a hidden agenda when it came to our family, so we kept away from them as much as we could.

"No," he responded, and as he straightened his back, it cracked, causing him to exhale softly. It was evident that he was trying to mask his pain. Of course, there were moments where he milked the opportunity to receive pity and special favours, but you'd always be able to tell which times were fake and which weren't. This time around, I could tell he wasn't faking, and my heart wept for him.

"Seriously Ayman you haven't seen her in forever, her daughter just died, show some respect" I pleaded.

"I don't want to go okay, and you can't make me!" his voice bellowed, he turned away from me then and slid back into his bed.

He was right, I couldn't make him, but I really wanted him to come. Just once I wanted to have a good time with my family, but it looked like we'd have to keep postponing that time for another day. I was angry with Yaba and looking at Ayman only made me more upset at him. His son, his only son, was in a crap ton of physical pain. I couldn't even begin to comprehend how lonely he must be. There wasn't another man around the house with whom he could speak. What was his world like when he needed advice that only a man could give? Or information about the changes he was going through as a teenager. It wasn't fair to him that he had to go through this alone, and as much as his sisters were there for him, I know he craved having a brother or father around. It seemed like everyone around me carried the burden of their own struggles so heavily, seeing the pain of another would only make them fold under the pain. I was no stranger to such burdens, but Farah had it pretty bad.

My aunt, Farah, recently had a baby in June who passed away a month later. It hit her hard and ever since her daughter's passing, she hasn't been the same. I figured the more family around her, the happier she'd be. Since Ilham was a resident advisor for the summer and Ayman decided to bury himself in the darkness of his room, the only family supporting my aunt would be Yuma, Nur and I...again.

Sighing, I headed into my room and changed. Looking at my reflection in the mirror I stood there and stared. I looked exhausted and depressed, the person staring back at me heavy with turmoil and silent agony but I had to pull myself together for Farah, so I mustered up the most genuine smile I could. The smile didn't reach my eyes; there contained no life behind it, no emotion, but it wasn't like she would notice. She was in her own world these days and wouldn't notice something as trivial as a forced smile. So, with a push, I put aside my self-hatred and headed downstairs and out the door where Yuma was waiting for me in her Jeep.

The music blared loudly from the car. Filling the air, the music overflowed and rushed out of the Jeep, onto the silent streets on which we resided. I once asked Yuma why she turned her music up so loud and she shrugged her shoulders.

Only when I continued to press her about it did she answer: "It stops me from thinking so much, I think too much about how my life has come to shit; I've done nothing with my life and seen nothing. I've only suffered, the music..it keeps me from thinking about wanting to end my life."

It scared me to hear her say things that were so serious, I loved her more than anything and anyone. A world without her was a world I didn't want to live in, regardless of whether she was depressed or not.

"Yuma, why don't you talk to me?" I pleaded. "Bond with me, studies show that speaking about what pains us or what's going on in our heads helps us. I get that you don't think therapy works because they don't understand us or our culture. But what about me? I understand, why don't you speak to me? You always say how you want a family and how you want to spend time with us. You have that chance, you have us right here and now, so talk to me. Please. You always promise to spend time with me, but you never do. Why is it so hard for you to talk to your own daughter, help me understand. Help me see what you see."

Yuma turned the volume up, I exhaled and buckled my seat belt. I rolled down my window and allowed the wind to caress my face. Of course, she wasn't going to respond; she never did. Nur sat in the back trying to sing along, but the Arabic words were going too fast for her to pick them up. She danced, nonetheless, and continued to talk about how she was going to play with her cousins with the excitement only a six-year-old could contain.

As Nur sang and danced, I thought of my aunt and how sad it was that her daughter had passed. I had held the baby once. She had struggled to breathe since her birth and seemed so fragile. Steadily, she continued losing weight. Her little body was so small and frail that I was terrified to touch her. I was afraid I'd bring her more harm than good, but my aunt had insisted for me to hold her.

I remember seeing the look of loss in Aunt Farah's face. A mother's intuition does seem to pick up everything about her children, for it appeared that she knew her daughter wouldn't be here long. It was just in the subtle way that she touched her daughter's hair or hummed to her softly when she cried out in need. It seemed that she knew. Although she couldn't do anything to stop God from taking her into His kingdom, she tried her best to enjoy the remaining moments she had left with her daughter.

I also thought back to the first years when Aunt Farah had arrived to the U.S. Her presence in our lives brought along its fair share of great times and beautiful memories. We showed her around Syracuse; she took everything in and made the comparison between the U.S. and hers--or better yet, ours, back east. At the end of the tour, it came as no surprise that her favorite place was McDonald's, and according to her, the one in Jerusalem wasn't as great as the ones in America. So there you have it--America was loved for what it does best: burgers and fries in the land of the super-sized.

At the time of her first visit, Aunt Farah was only allowed to stay with us temporarily for three months; that is unless she was to find a husband and marry successfully, but none of us foresaw that happening right away. We were content with her company and didn't want to waste what little time we had then, by searching for suitors.

Aunt Farah would sit with us into the late hours of the night alongside Yuma, who happened to be a terrible translator with her broken English. It was a rare sight to see Yuma happy, and when she was around Farah she seemed to be the happiest.

We introduced Aunt Farah to all of our family and friends. It wasn't until she met Abbas that she found what is now her husband. I remember the day they first met, just how she looked back at him with a smile on her face, as we were pulling out of his garage. Yuma scolded her, by saying that she looked too desperate in staring back, given that it was no secret she had to leave back to Palestine soon. But the late night talks we had with her gave away how much she really liked the man. She'd spend hours putting her outfit together, asking us kids for our advice on the matter, even though at that age Yuma still dressed us. We thought nothing of it then, but the days before her engagement to Abbas proved to be some of our best, even to this day. She'd brought new life to our small and empty apartment, breathing energy into our once dull routine. Her humor was refreshing and her love for all things American made you see this country in a much different light.

It scares me how remembering the happiest of moments can make your heart ache or clench in your chest with a longing. Such memories make me wish that I could spend just one more day in the past, to relive and linger in that moment that has seared itself into the folds of my brain with fondness.

We take for granted the good times as we live and breathe them. Only once it becomes history, do we wish to repeat those moments. Then and only then, do we allow history to live within the present. I finally understood why Yuma hated remembering the past; it can hurt more to remember than to forget.

CHAPTER 4

Foster

"Strength does not come from winning. Your struggles
develop your strengths. When you go through hardships
and decide not to surrender, that is strength."

– Arnold Schwarzenegger

We tend to forget the memories that our subconscious believes
is too traumatic for us to keep within the forefront of our
tapped memories. Where do these memories go? How do they return
to us? How do we retrieve that kind of memory? What do we do when
it's revealed? And how do we deal with the revelation once it shows its
face to us?

Buried away were memories I concealed long ago, memories that I
did not recall until a small trigger opened the floodgates, and I found
myself drowning in memories that were once familiar and now seem
like a clip from a movie. I recalled the dark and cold attic where Ilham
and I slept, the scrutiny Yuma was under during the days we were sent
away, the unfamiliarity of a house filled with rules, and children I wasn't

accustomed to. I pondered for weeks, wondering if anything would ever be the same for my siblings and I.

"Sweetie, did your mom do this to you?" asked the woman whose office I was currently seated in. She was one of the many guidance counselors assigned to the 1st grade and by far the sweetest. I looked down to what she was pointing at, the bruises that were covering my legs which were now blue and green. It was spring; Ilham and I wanted to wear dresses to school. We didn't think that the bruises were a big deal. Bruises were just a part of being beaten all the time, and seeing our bodies filled with them didn't mean much to us--not anymore, at least.

"Did what?" I asked, a little confused. She sat one leg over the other with a kind smile upon her face. Moving closer to me, she bent down and used her pencil to point at the bruises on my leg.

"Where did these come from? Don't worry, you aren't in trouble. I just want to help you, and I can't do that if I don't know how you got them. Don't you want me to help you?"

"Yea..." I responded, confused. How and why she wanted to help me, I didn't know. She didn't know us, she wasn't in our family, so why did someone who didn't know me want to help me when I wasn't their blood relative?

"Did your dad do this?" she asked, eyes wide with concern. I shook my head no and she continued down the list of relatives that could possibly do this,

"How about your mom? Does she know who did this?"

I looked at her confused then, "Well yea, of course she knows."

"What do you mean, sweetie?" Her eyebrows furrowed together in confusion. "Why did you say that she knew?"

"Well..." I started swinging my legs in the chair, "she did it."

The counselor immediately started writing things down on her note-pad before heading to her desk. "Give me a second Amani, okay? I'll be right back," she informed me before leaving the room.

Before it dawned on me what was happening, Ilham was brought down to the room and we were instructed to sit quietly and wait for some-one they called "social workers" to arrive. Scared, I looked to Ilham and asked her what was going on. She gave me a menacing stare before whis-pering harshly, "Stupid! What did you say to them?"

I cowered in her gaze, "Nothing, I didn't say anything."

"What did they ask you?!" she demanded,

"She asked me if Yuma knew about the bruises and I said, 'Yea, because she did them.' She said she couldn't help me unless she knew. She was really sweet Ilham."

"Of course she was! She wanted to get Yuma in trouble, and now because of you we won't see her anymore!"

With tears pooling my line of sight, fear overcame me as I pondered what would happen to Yuma. Was she going where Alzalim was? Would they be together? Who would bring us to see them? Would he be mad at me?

"I don't want Yuma to get in trouble. I didn't mean for this to hap-pen wallah!"

Ilham rolled her eyes and sighed, "There's nothing we can do now; we'll just have to deal with whatever happens."

The memory fades away. I willed the memory to materialize over and over again, trying to remember anything else that happened within the confines of that office, but I wore myself out recalling this particular incident. There wasn't a paper trail left that could give me any clues or jog my memory of what happened next, but some of the gaps of that period started to fill up over time.

The unwelcoming touch of fall's cold hand ran up my spine causing a series of shudders to erupt before I clenched my blanket closer. Its uninviting presence lingered over me as it entered my pores and nestled its way into the marrow of my bones. The cold wasn't leaving and it pulled me from the landscapes of dreams I was creating. I opened my eyelids to see Ilham asleep right across from me. I smiled, happy to be with her in this place. Being away from Ayman was hard enough, so I was glad she was around to look after me. This place would have been ten times scarier without her here.

Looking around, the place did give fear a run for its money. The attic we were assigned to sleep in was massive. The ceilings had no end, and I couldn't see the end of the room--it seemed to go on forever. Most of the attic was engulfed in darkness, and the dark blue carpeting didn't do the light any favors. There were only the two beds Ilham and I were sleeping on; the dresser between us kept the few clothes we managed to pack within it. Parallel to our beds was the window that allowed the cold to come rushing in with its loud and uncomfortable presence. That morning, I stared out the window from within the confines of my bed--too afraid to close it, yet curious as to why it was open.

I hadn't been counting the days; the separation from Yuma bore its weight heavily on my conscience. I didn't intend for us to be ripped away from her--didn't mean to make her seem like an unfit mother to the world. All I understood from the bits and pieces Ilham could gather and make sense of herself was that Yuma had to fight to get us back, since there was evidence against her suggesting she hadn't treated us well.

Being at the foster home was so different to our home life, that I couldn't fully grasp the rules. For example, at the foster home, whenever we did something we weren't supposed to, we were 'grounded', as in, we weren't allowed any special privileges or rewards. Back home, whenever we did something wrong Yuma would hit us until our skin turned red, make us eat jalapenos as if she was grating them with our teeth slammed shut until our taste buds would scream in agony, or simply force sriracha down our throats--which burned its way down into the pit of our stomach, until we threw up. Although unconventional, we learned our lessons with Yuma's punishments rather than the fickle and carefree methods we were given in the foster home.

They were kind in a different manner than one would be accustomed to, they were kind because they pitied us. Not just us but all the girls in the home, they saw us as broken and forgotten leaving you feeling exposed. I didn't like it. Didn't like it one bit.

Sadly, I don't remember anything after that point. I was too young to hold onto much else of our time in the group home. Flashbacks of these memories came and went. One moment, my mind would take me there to relive those memories, and the next I'd be with Yuma at home.

I thought of asking her about it again, but I knew she'd say what she always said, "I don't remember anything." That was a lie. She just didn't like remembering her past or speaking of it for that matter. She hated the parts of her brain that allowed her to store memories, wishing instead that she could forget things as they happen. Refusing to even reminisce over photos or join in on conversations about recollected adventures we had as children. How much pain does someone need to be in to stick to such a demanding rule.

On this particular day, Aunt Farah walked into the room Yuma and I were in--I wondered if she knew about the time Ilham and I were in the group home, or anything else that pertained to us being taken away from Yuma. A part of me knew that if Yuma wanted something to remain unspoken, it would remain that way--against my better judgement, I approached the topic. I needed to know more about our time there. Ilham, being only a year older, most likely wouldn't remember much either.

It annoyed me that I couldn't remember more, that I couldn't recall moments that shaped me, as a young child growing up. I wanted to reach those memories that I blocked out. *What memories were far too traumatic that my growing brain thought it best to erase my time there?* Forgetting to erase the memories I did recall from the recesses of my mind, I knew the younger me would be very upset that all traces of that time were now gone from the history etched between the wrinkles and folds within my brain.

Whatever the rest was impacted the development of my behaviour, so much so that a year later, in the second grade, an incident happened that influenced me to cover up the truth.

It was yet another boring night where I had nothing at all to do, Ayman was busy playing his Nintendo and Ilham and I were fighting which meant we'd ignore one another for the rest of the day. The TV had been out of commission for a few days now and usually there were a select few channels to watch that didn't cost Yuma a dime. Shows like Zoboomafoo, Arthur, Dragon Tails, Teletubbies, and Pokémon played reruns all throughout the week to keep us and many other poor families entertained.

Yuma was able to get someone to come and fix the television for us, but my patience was running thin, since that person was repairing the tv for hours. I was growing restless with the need for something to do.

"Yuma I'm bored" I complained, but she paid no mind to me. I rolled around on the floor repeating my complaint, "Yuma I'm so bored!"

The repairman grunted as he tried squeezing his frame behind the TV set. Yuma watched over his work, curious as to what he was doing. Knowing that we had no money and no man in the house at the time, I gathered she was studying the tools he used as well as the accessories needed to replace the damage. She liked to learn from any situation just in case we found ourselves in the same predicament again, in order to rely on

30

herself. Yuma was a very smart woman for someone who knew no English and lived in a foreign country for less than 8 years. It was her ability to observe that allowed her to learn and acquire many skills without asking for help.

"Yuma I'm bored!!" I screamed and whined. Frustrated with my complaining, she picked up a CD, turned to me and yelled, "Khalas!! (Stop!!),", chucking the CD at me in frustration, the cd went flying rapidly in my direction and sliced the left side of my nose in half. I felt air rush in, touching parts of my bare skin that was unaccustomed to its presence. The flap of my nose slightly dangling over my lip. Blood slowly crept down my lips and dripped off my chin with urgency. I couldn't see the full extent of the damage, nor did I want to. All I knew was the pain, how loud it was, how it demanded to be felt. Funny thing about pain isn't it? How it comes without warning or without noise, yet its pain is so loud that you can't help but cover your ears in agony at its fury.

I rose to my legs in a panic, holding my hands in front of my face I blocked its view from the repairman, "Yuma!!!" I screamed crying now, "Yuma help me!!!"

Rushing to my side Yuma started freaking out, Arabic words poured from her mouth in a frenzy while she grabbed a clean hand towel and covered my nose.

"Yala, yala (come on)" she cooed leading me into the bathroom. Turning the faucet on she drenched the towel in water before wiping the blood off my face. It was everywhere, an ocean of red waves filled the sink with blotches covering the surrounding area in globs.

"Now lift your head up and keep it all the way bent back" she ordered in our native tongue.

"Okay" was all I could get out before she cut in,

"You're so stupid, why would you do this to yourself! How could you do this to yourself! I told you to be careful and you never listen to me"

Confused I looked at her, "YOU did this, not me!"

Her eyes grew darker then, clenching my arms she whispered in a low and superior tone, "You're going to tell anyone that asks you that you did this to yourself, you understand? Take responsibility for what you did, you shouldn't be in the same room as a man you know better! This is what happens when you don't listen."

With this new knowledge I didn't dare speak against her, she was my mother, her word was law. She knew best. She knew things I didn't and would never do anything to intentionally harm us. Everything was a learning lesson, but this wasn't something she taught me. This was a lesson that the cards of cause and effect taught me, something I had to take responsibility for.

"I...I did this...I cut my nose" I agreed, enlightened as to my deed. Closing my eyes, I cursed this position, I couldn't risk any more attention from school given the last incident and being taken away from Yuma. I didn't want anyone to blame or harass her, not my teachers or Siti.

The memory of Yuma cleaning my nose before getting me stitched up remained with me.

"Why would you do this to yourself? Do you hate yourself this much? Or do you just not think before you do anything?" she asked. Her voice began fading out as she dabbed the wound. I sat there quietly, not listening as she continued to drone on, "How many times do I tell you not to harm your face, it's what will get you a handsome husband one day. No one wants an ugly wife."

I was dazed and numb from painkillers the next day in class as I sat at my desk with my nose wrapped in bandages. My fellow classmates were unable to turn their gazes away from the sight of me. No one asked me anything--too afraid I guess. It wasn't until my second-grade teacher walked in did she drop everything and approach me. "Oh my goodness Amani are you okay?"

I looked at her then; her blue eyes and blonde hair were so inviting and bright. She was the coolest teacher I had thus far. I enjoyed learning from her.

"Amani I just want to help you and I can't do that if you don't tell me how you got this" she cooed.

I looked her in her eyes then, eyes that showed a wealth of concern. Once more I was faced with someone who cared about me, someone who wasn't related to me by blood or name. There weren't any strings attaching us and yet she cared, why? Why did people pretend to care when all they wanted to do was rip those from you that truly did care about your wellbeing? What was the urgency in that kind of behaviour? What reward did it offer them? Did they think that things would magically solve themselves? What if things became even worse? There was no way of knowing. I had no clue. But I knew one thing, she wouldn't be allowed to take away the woman who did care about me, the one woman who, despite all her challenges loved us the way she knew best.

"I won't let them take me from her; not again, Yuma was the reason why I was alive today," I thought to myself.

"I did it," I said. "I was reckless and didn't look out for myself properly." I didn't flinch--didn't hesitate. I couldn't be the reason we were taken from Yuma again. I needed to be the soldier this time and brave my wounds without shame, but rather, with honor.

I was a survivor in a world I wasn't meant to live in, to begin with. I was told that I was born a premature baby--that the doctor told Yuma I wasn't going to live. And in saying so, Yuma never came to see me at the hospital, while I fought for my life.

I fit in the palm of their hand--my parents told me. I was the smallest thing they'd ever seen. I wasn't supposed to live and yet, after two months in the hospital, I was able to go home with an apnea monitor that measured the progress of my heart and breathing pattern. If at any point it detected something amiss, the alarm would sound, and I would be checked on to be sure I was alive and breathing.

"We hardly slept; we were so afraid that if we slept too long we'd miss the chance to stimulate your heart into beating and we'd lose you," Alzalim once told me. "It was the most stressful part about being a parent--your life was literally in our hands. It was scary."

All in all, I was the child that survived when all believed I wouldn't; I was a survivor. I'd braved every obstacle set against me since the moment of my birth. I needed to persist in withstanding anything attempting to pull me apart or break me. I refused to allow anyone the chance to rip my siblings and I from our home once more, and so I stared back, intensely and intently--with Yuma's panicked face flashing in my mind as she frantically tried stopping the blood from flowing out of my face.

I remembered how Yuma scolded me for doing this to myself, trying to persuade a young child that they were to blame rather than herself--I recalled the fear that overcame her, knowing she messed up big time. This wasn't like the time when she threatened to boil us and eat us. . .or when she twisted our ears so hard that she split it at the crease, causing it to bleed. Nor was it like when she chased us around the house with a spoon, so hot, I could have sworn that lava had seared its mark on my wrist. This time she wasn't able to hide the wounds inflicted on me--it sat there plainly on my face wrapped in gauze, noticeable to everyone in its path.

I needed to protect us; a soldier does what is needed for the greater good, no matter the wounds they bare. "Like I said Mrs. Zillow, I did it to myself."

CHAPTER 5

Soulless

"That's the thing about depression: A human being
can survive almost anything, as long as she sees the
end in sight. But depression is so insidious, and it
compounds daily, that it's impossible to ever see
the end. The fog is like a cage without a key."

– Elizabeth Wurtzel

S itting on the couch at my aunt's place I stared at the flat screen that
sat above the fireplace she never used. What was it about Arabians
spending the extra bucks on a house for a fireplace if they weren't plan-
ning on using it? I couldn't help but think about my future then, after
college I was most likely going to grad school out of Syracuse so that I
can escape the prison that I've been born and bred into.

I didn't like Syracuse; the winters were too depressing, and the sum-
mers, were too humid. There wasn't a balance in nature, as if the universe just disliked the city as well. It was a city full of retired individuals;
I wouldn't coin it a "young people" city. Had it not been for LeMoyne
College, Onondaga Community College and Syracuse University, I

don't think there would be any young adults at all. It was a city that survived on the influx of college students who returned from their summer vacations and during those months it's as if the city prepares itself, in advance. Special school deals, promotions, coupons, two for ones--no promotion seemed to be spared--to me, it was sad and honestly, kind of desperate.

I wanted to travel and settle down in a place that was like spring all year long. A place where the breeze was just the right temperature and the sun bronzed you in just the right way. I needed to be in a place filled with opportunity, a place where there was always something to do, no matter the hour--a place that gave you hope and made you want to hustle and work. Syracuse wasn't that city.

"Amani?" My aunt cooed, shaking my head so that I was back to consciousness. I looked up to see her eyeing me with concern written all over her face.

"Yea, what's up?"

She sat beside me as she cleaned up the mess her children made. "You always look sad, like you hate your life"

I laughed then, "I always look sad; what's new?"

She frowned, "It hurts your mother to see you guys all so sad. She works hard to make sure there's a roof over your heads, which takes all the energy to be able to spend time and talk with you all."

Farah was a beautiful woman, although she did carry the biggest head I've ever seen. Her cheekbones were high and sharp, with skin as tight as her thin lips. Naturally she was bronzed from the Palestine sun, with massively big eyes that gave her a regal look. All in all she was a contrasting beauty to Yuma.

I sighed, "Yea, well, to be honest, even if she did have all the time in the world to spend with us, she'd still be in bed watching Arab Idol. He took any life she had in her; she's got nothing left. I love her so much

Khalto, all I want is to be able to make her smile. Someday I'll make her proud. Mark my words."

She gave me a weak smile; I could see she barely slept, considering how dark her eyes were and the stress lines becoming permanent along her eyes and forehead. Reaching over, I hugged her tightly, "Everything's going to be okay, with time."

Khalto Farah cried then, letting the rain of her clouded eyes dance on my shoulder. I wish I knew the right words to say, but losing a daughter a month after she was born was something hard to recover from. They aren't like any one of us. Babies have yet to commit any sins or gain an enemy--Nurrah was purely innocent, so why did she have to suffer?

"I just don't understand why this happened, I think about her everyday," Khalto Farah cried.

"I know you do, but God tests his toughest warriors. The harder the test, the greater the love. I know it sounds absurd but how can you see who's faithful and who isn't ya know? The greatest thing in your life are your children, right? Since you had to take pills and undergo so many tests to be able to have them. And the only thing Yuma ever wanted was true and unwavering love. But what was she given? An American Arab who couldn't love her the way she deserved because they were two culturally different Arabs of the same land. Plus, he's a felon who created a family with her and then abandoned her--he could care less about her and us right? Our deepest desires are being used to test our faith. Trust in God, and everything will be clear to you one day. Just have faith."

"I can't" she sobbed, "I don't have the energy to pray."

I said nothing then; for that was the response my mother had always given me when I tried convincing her to pray again. I felt wrong because I didn't pray, but I had wanted to get back to it. Reconnecting with God was a plan long overdue. Without faith, it's easy to lose sight of one's purpose and strength.

Yuma walked in then and told my aunt to suck it up--that crying wasn't going to bring her child back, and there was nothing she'd benefit from by torturing herself. Farah rolled her eyes as she dried them.

My mother was brutal, but she was right which is why her younger sister didn't argue with her. Khalto Farah just turned to me and said, "I hate your father, he took any ounce of kindness out of her."

I half smiled. Farah was right, but my father had taken far more than her kindness away. I truly believed that he had taken her soul by the time he left.

I thought about how I was born a premature. Those who were there dubbed me, "the miracle child," saying I had all the odds stacked against me, yet I lived. Even as I was brought into the world, my doctor told my mom there was a very low likelihood that I'd survive. I felt connected in a way to Farah's lost daughter. She and I were warriors; we had fought to live. I felt that I needed to honor her by living. She battled daily to remain here with us, so it wasn't fair that I was taking my life for granted.

On our way back home I looked at Yuma. She looked worn out and depressed--a look she's had longer than I can remember.

"Yuma?"

"What?" she responded, annoyed as she lowered the volume of the music. She hated when anyone spoke to her while she listened to her music.

"You should show Khalto Farah a little more compassion; I mean just because Yaba hurt you doesn't mean you should be mean to everyone around you."

"Amani, shut up okay? You don't know anything, so don't tell me what I need to do--I am your mom."

I quickly transitioned into being annoyed, "Okay your attitude is not necessary, and people treat you the way you treat them."

"Don't talk to me like that! Respect me! I'm your mother, you're not mine!"

"Then start acting like it, being a mother is more than just paying bills so that we have a roof over our heads; what's the point in having children if you don't get to know them? You can't blame us for being alive or punish us OR make us feel guilty that we're alive. You decided to have children so it's a requirement that you raise them. You spend all of your free time with Khalto or watching TV on your phone when you could be spending time with your own kids who actually want to spend time with you."

"Amani be quiet!!" she yelled full of anger. My cheek burned. It dawned on me then that she slapped me, acid like and cold. Turning the music up so that my ears now felt like they were bleeding was the tell-tale sign that this conversation was over. That's how our conversations ended, always. Cradling my cheek, I stared out the window, eyes filled with unshed tears. This life of mine was a joke and I didn't understand God's humor in writing it like this.

The very next day my heart dropped. It was a morning that started off like all the others but took a sudden dramatic turn once the afternoon rolled in. I was lying on my bed with a book in hand, escaping reality as I so often did so that I could temporarily live in a world where I could let myself go. Days like these were quiet, the air still, the streets clear and the atmosphere completely calm. It allowed me to relish in the beauty of the books I would read. It would only take a minor rift, though, to disrupt serene days like these where almost like a rippling effect, we were destined to repeat history and face it once again.

"Amani!" Ayman called out, his voice filled with panic and a tad bit of fear.

My heartbeat rose in speed, adrenaline rushing through my veins. I wondered what would cause such emotion to arise from my brother, which he also barely seemed to contain lately. Getting out of bed, I hurried downstairs to see my brother just staring at his phone. Heading over to him, I asked him what was wrong.

When he responded all I could hear was a loud ringing in my ears. "Yaba is back." As he looked up from his phone, fear was written all over my face too.

CHAPTER 6

Him

"If you know the enemy and know yourself you
need not fear the results of a hundred battles."

– Sun Tzu

W hile sitting down on the couch, my heart went on overdrive.
There was no way he could be back--it should be impossible.
Not too long ago, he was in Arizona where he went in and out of jail
over his petty crimes. Why did they let him out? Why should anyone
here care that he was back? He caused nothing but drama and violence
wherever he went.

Bad business--Alzalim was nothing but bad business and ruined
credit. The sound of the clock ticking filled my ears. I experienced
such fierce tunnel vision that my brother had to shake me out of
my thoughts.

"What?" I asked, making eye contact with him.

He slowly sat beside me trying not to show the pain he was in.
"What's wrong?"

I sighed, "Nothing, I just don't want him back, Ayman. There's going to be a lot of fighting and a lot more drama than we need."

I noticed an ant crawled its way into our home and around our space, climbing over the bumpy roads of carpet it faced to reach the kitchen where it would scavenge food to bring back to its colony. I thought back to how I felt this morning when I woke up--my biggest dilemma was deciding whether or not I wanted to reread an old book or get on *Wattpad* to read something overly done that was in no way believable.

I never imagined that I'd be worried about my father coming back since he seemed to have finally gotten what he wanted--his freedom away from us. He'd broken away from his burden, his chains and had set himself free, removing all ties he had with us, including Nur. So why was he back? What was left for him here? Did he want to come back to see the damage he had left--how the kids he helped create were living a sad and depressing life? I didn't understand what could possibly possess him to feel the need to drop into the city.

"Why is he back?" I asked, looking at Ayman as he yawned and stretched the bones that made up his body.

"I don't know for sure; he said something about being allowed back until his court date in October."

Court date? Oh, right! He did have a court date that he needed to attend for a number of the crimes he was booked for in Arizona. But I didn't understand why they'd let him leave the state if he was under such scrutiny.

Exhaling softly, I rubbed my aching eyes, wishing I had moved back into my dorm for the year, to avoid running into him. The dorms' move in date was only a week away; had I signed up, in just one week I would've rid myself of this sad reality I would now be forced to endure. I would have delved into studying and late-night shifts flipping burgers for privileged students.

I could tell that my anxiety was slowly making its way back happily into the dorm room of my body, looking over my shoulder being the returning habit that would make its debut once more. I felt terrible for Yuma mostly, she wouldn't be thrilled upon hearing the news, not at all.

"Oh and he's got a girlfriend apparently," Ayman added, dropping the biggest shocker Yaba's arrival carried with it. I watched as Ayman placed frozen hot pockets into the microwave oven.

My jaw still felt like it had dropped. "A what?! How in the world did he manage that?!"

"I don't know, she takes care of him apparently."

I grimaced at the thought of someone taking care of *him*. It grossed me out, knowing how filthy he was. Shuddering, I responded, "Ugh I don't know what woman would be willing and naïve enough to take care of a man like that."

"Her and Yuma apparently."

I scoffed before making feigned retching noises, "Apparently."

It always surprised me how my father managed to get any girl he wanted. I mean, honestly, the guy doesn't even look the part and he hasn't brushed his teeth in like three years! Women just don't have standards these days.

Looking out the window afraid that, at any moment, he'd pull up and stir drama up before the news that he was here settled in, brought worry to the creases in my forehead. I moaned internally in frustration. Not only did we have to deal with our good for nothing father, but his sister arrived from Palestine this summer to visit their family. That would have been perfectly fine, except that she brought all eight of her kids--the eldest being either fifth teen or sixth teen, I wasn't too sure. Arabs generally birthed mass amounts of kids early on in their marriage all at once and then raised the petting zoo they manifested, until one day their investment would turn around and aid them when they became too old to function. She was always a sweet and fun-loving woman. I was sad to not be able to see her more often.

"I don't know why you care so much, he's got a girlfriend so he isn't going to bother us," Ayman stated, matter of factly, into the microwave that hummed softly. I wish I knew what thoughts were going through his mind right now. I knew this situation would affect him the most considering he's always wanted the attention from our father more than any of us. Being the only boy left him stranded in this household.

Ayman never really knew what it was like to have a father figure or a best friend that could teach him what it meant to be a man or how to even become one. He never complained though, knowing that it wouldn't change anything. As his movements became less fluid and more exhausted over time, he seemed to lose the need to socialize or speak with others. I sensed his longing, though; even as he said our father's name, I knew he wanted those glowing moments with his dad, playing catch or laughing about an inside joke meant for just the two of them. The situation caused me to worry over his mental stability, how loved he felt, or how successful he'd become in the future. There were so many dangerous outcomes and possibilities that I hoped God would spare him from. After all, it was hard to hear that your own father plays catch with his nephews and takes them on exciting adventures rather than yourself, his own flesh and blood. That alone makes me weep for my brother.

Ayman struggled to push his back straighter than the hunch it was in, his face registering pain, but he didn't complain as he let his breath exhale from his distressed body. His eyes looked so sad, he looked life-less....he looked so much like Yuma, causing my heart to go out to him. He didn't deserve this--any of it. All I wanted to see was that big grin with teeth of various sizes and the smell of *Swedish Fish* filling the air.

His innocence dancing beside the harmony of a child's laughter in the sun's rays.

There was a time when Ayman smiled as much as I did and ran around the house...spending time with Ilham and I. When I think back to my childhood, the emotions I remember the most were happiness. The world seemed at peace then--quiet and calm. It was never too hot, and the winters never seemed too cold. Every morning when I opened the door, a bird's song would float in, flutter about, and leave me with the world's fullest smile.

I can still recall the breeze rushing in and tickling my little ears. Indeed it was calm back then. I can remember the rustling of papers as my two siblings and I quietly scribbled and let our imaginations soar while Yuma lay asleep in bed. Time was still, as we cut and pasted pieces upon pieces of paper to build trinkets to our heart's content. Technology never fancied our interest; our eyes were glued to the wonders we were creating. It was quite invigorating really, thinking about the completion of your work--about the masterpieces your mind formed. We were happy then, always linked by the arms and trailing one another. Our imaginations within the atmosphere we kept around us was palpable--the hopes and dreams we carried, brimming in our eyes. You could see the imagination without having to look very far.

When I think back I can remember those moments filled with light. I can only remember those calm days and gentle nights. I can remember seeing the world with eager eyes, wanting to see more. They say that as you get older, the light leaves you and the harsh realities of life set in draining the hopes and dreams from within you. I wish I could be the one to challenge that, but I can't. I lost my light, my flame a mere flicker. The laughter nothing but a memory; the imagination...sucked dry. No longer are we linked; no longer are we creating. No longer are we happy--instead, we are each walking our own paths of sadness and grief. We've turned away from those who are our family because no one cares enough to ask the other how they were holding up. Were we even a family to begin with? Or was my imagination so powerful that I managed to convince myself that we were truly happy?

Today we are glued to the screens of false light while the sidewalks remain empty. No imagination scribbled on the sidewalks, no singing and chanting from children as they hopscotch through neighboring blocks. No sign of life, anywhere. What will become of our happiness? Where is the family I once had? The bond we once glued together? The love we once showcased without hesitation? You know, when I think back to my childhood the only emotion I can remember is happiness.

"Amani" Ayman called out. I felt my consciousness fading back in and turned my gaze back to him. Moving aside, I let him pass by me with the lingering smell of pizza flavoured pocket treats flooding my nostrils. I watched him walk away with the kink in his hip accompanying his laboured breathing. The sun shone brightly today, reaching inside our home slowly to wrap its arm around him and help Ayman up the stairs.

How can one man cause so much pain and destruction to the foundation of this family? And why did he decide to come back when we were doing just fine without him?

CHAPTER 7

8th Grade Surprise

"Happiness is not something you postpone for the future;
it is something you design for the present."

– Jim Rohn

*W*e awoke for school that morning by the early morning sunrise.
*The air was chilly, leaving a wet residue in the atmosphere and on
everything it touched. The smell of last night's rain lingered heavily in the
air; it was one of those days that made you want to stay in bed, but Yuma
wasn't having it with our fake coughs.*

*Stepping out of bed, my sister made her way to the bathroom to brush
her teeth while I stretched my sleeping muscles awake. Our apartment
was empty; there was a kitchen, a bathroom, three bedrooms, and three
living rooms of various sizes. We owned one couch and four donated beds
that we were incredibly thankful for--personally, sleeping on the floor had
begun to hurt my back way too much. Our house was empty then, without
much food to keep us going. It's crazy how I had a bunch of extended family who owned grocery stores, cell phone stores, and car dealerships with
a steady flow of income coming in...yet they wouldn't help their family*

in need. My mom was right, they only cared about money and gaining more power and influence over others. Love wasn't a term they recognized without conditions.

I sighed. Although we didn't have many things or clothes that other kids had, we knew that our luck would one day change because our father would be home with us to change things for the better. There was a saying that I would tell my parents, "Although we are not rich in wealth, we are rich in love and that's all that matters."

Yuma was up early today; her beautiful face lit up the house and warmed my thawing body. "Guess who's coming home today?" she asked with much excitement.

I yawned before looking at her curiously. "Who is?"

"Your dad! He's coming home from prison today to stay with us!"

"For how long?" Ayman asked tilting his head to the side, confused.

She gave a slight smile, "For good; he's staying with us for good this time."

Ilham, Ayman and I all stared at one another in shock - there was no way!! It was too good to be true!! I rushed to the window and pushed the curtain aside. Looking out the glass square, I sketched every detail of the view in my memory. I wanted to remember this day forever--the day Yaba finally comes home to us. Two birds fluttered a bit further away, chasing one another through the sky before settling into a tree. The sun was finally heading into its usual position in the sky. But today it was different; no longer did the day seem gloomy and drained. It was being reborn...the night's rain washing away the troubles of yesterday and wiping the Earth clean for today so that we could begin anew without our past sins clouding the new slate given to us, our second chance at a family.

Inhaling softly, I couldn't contain myself, I was too excited to come home from school today. I would finally be able to embrace Yaba the way a father and daughter should be allowed to, without time limits, without guards, without other prisoners around. No wired fences ruining the beauty of an embrace between family. No walls of washed beige giving way to the prisons age, where even the prison itself seemed devoid of any life. He would be free to hug me as long as he'd like, pick me up and toss me into the air the way the commercials show it dramatically done. I would be able to see him dressed up in suits and ties, watch him shave in the morning alongside Ayman who eagerly waited for puberty to bring him the beard of his dreams on a golden platter. But most importantly, I would be able to walk beside in public, holding his chain free hands, letting the world know that he was my father and I was his daughter.

The day seemed to drag on in class; sitting at my desk, the clock and I seemed to be in what was a staring competition with an unspoken rule that, if I were to blink, time would drag on even more slowly keeping me trapped in these walls that were supposed to educate us. Education, that consisted of what was socially acceptable and what was not--the progress of white supremacy and the oppression of people of color. Education, of how America is the "land of the free." As if it weren't hard enough that I was a Muslim in a white prioritized and favoured educational institution.

"Amani to the office please, Amani to the office," the overhead speakers connected throughout the building announced. Sitting up, I looked around as others in my class peered at me. Deciding I didn't want to be the center of attention any longer, I gathered my belongings and headed out into the hall toward the main office. When I entered, Ilham and Yuma were waiting for me.

Before saying anything, Ilham piped up and answered before I even knew what I was going to ask: "We're going home early because Yaba is home."

I smiled then. I would finally be able to see my dad in the setting he was supposed to be in. No child should ever have to grow up seeing their dad in prison--it forces them to grow up too soon. Seeing the harsh realities of life early on makes the innocence they're supposed to carry wash away, being given a picture book of reality and the consequences that befall bad decisions. It made children feel that prison was home in a way, becoming so used to the protocol and the environment if they were to end up there one day, they'd feel less inclined to want to change their lives because they understood what life was like on the inside already. Prison should never be the teaching ground of children.

"Let's go, he's waiting for us at home with Ayman" Yuma ordered, with excitement in her step; I followed quickly behind with Ilham. The smell of Yuma's Heavenly perfume marked the special occasion. I smiled, knowing that whenever she wore that perfume it meant we were going to have a good day. She so rarely wore that perfume that I smiled my brightest, because I knew that it was a special day in which she felt good.

When we arrived home, it felt as if the front door would never grow closer; the excitement rushed through the static of energy in the atmosphere. How many days had we counted? How many moments of sadness and grief had we felt when others had looked at us and whispered words of disgrace our way, because there wasn't a man at home taking care of us. Those in our community had shunned us because we didn't have money or status to embellish our names. We were jokes to them--a reminder of what the fall from grace would look like: a poverty-stricken family with no furniture and no man at home. We were close to wild animals in their eyes.

I held my breath and pushed open the door...the rooms blurred by as Ilham and I scanned and hurried past them when we didn't see him in there. The kitchen was the last stop. Rushing to the edge of the door, we both stopped and caught our breaths: He was sitting at the table with Ayman on his lap, drawing what looked like Mickey Mouse. I smiled then--it was so picturesque! The sun crawled in, touching Alzalim and Ayman, so that their shadows were cast across the kitchen floor at the edge of our feet...just at the kitchen's entrance, enticing us in.

When he turned around, it seemed to me like he was doing it all in slow motion. Dropping his pencil to the table then, pushing aside the drawing that was now officially the past collecting dust to be returned to at another time and replayed to relive this moment again. His body moved to face us, and then it happened, we made eye contact. It happened then and there, in the privacy of our own home and with that we smiled.

I tell ya, there was a time when I could smile so wide for my father that nothing could remove it. My love for him was so strong and my pride ran so deep that I'd flaunt it whenever I had the opportunity to. Time really does a lot to a relationship, to a family, and to the development of a person. It seems like forever ago that I once felt love for him--such an unknown emotion whenever I think of him now.

"Hey Yaba," I said softly, dazed.

"Hey habibti."

I tell ya, there was a time when I had a smile so wide for my father. The glow of it bounced off me, showcasing the pride I had to be his daughter...to carry his last name through the growth of my childhood and upon my identity as I aged. I looked upon him as our saviour, when in reality, he brought about our destruction.

As a child I could not see the politics behind the suffering he caused Yuma because she did such a wonderful job of hiding it from us. She never wanted us to hate our father or disrespect him so she kept her struggles from us and instead let us believe she was the wrongdoer in our family dynamic. Even as we stomped around screaming, "We want Yaba!" when Yuma said we weren't allowed anything due to the fact we were poor, she never confessed that it was because she was giving him most of our money to support him while in prison. The entire time she let us believe she was the criminal in our lives so that our perception of him wouldn't be skewed. She prayed that with her careful handling of his image in our minds, he'd come home and fit like that puzzle piece we've needed for so long. Time revealed everything eventually, and in witnessing the damage he wrought over the years to come did my hate grow for him. She could no longer sugar coat the truth and with the bitter taste of reality came our undying devotion to Yuma vowing to protect her when there was no one else who could.

CHAPTER 8

QTNA

"Life is rife with frustrations, jealousies and, on occasion, an overwhelming sense of its injustices, but it's a big mistake to let such negative sentiments rule our lives and dictate choices."

– Mariella Frostrup

A few days after hearing the news of Alzalim's return to Syracuse, Ayman and I were lounging around while Yuma was at work. Ever since she heard the news, Yuma would not let the issue drop.

"Call your grandmother to see how long he's staying" she ordered. "Call your father, see if his girlfriend answers," she asked at another time. "Call your grandmother house and see if your father girlfriend answers," was another request. "Can you believe your grandmother let a woman who isn't your father's wife sleep in her house?!" She finally exclaimed. "He's so ugly, ugly, ugly!"

"WE KNOW YUMA" Ayman and I would reply simultaneously. It was sad to see our dear mother in such a state, but it was also getting annoying.

She'd ask us to Google him and see if his court date information would just pop up as a Google suggestion. *Did you mean "find out detailed information about Alzalim's court date to appease your mom's frustrations and jealousy?"* Why yes Google, that is exactly what I'm looking for!

She'd sit and wonder aloud what his new girlfriend looked like and if he loved her.

"Yuma just move on and get the divorce already!" I told her frustrated one night when she came home from work, "It's annoying to see you so distraught over a man that never loved you in the first place!"

She sat silently that night. Her usual cup of coffee lay sitting in her hand as its aroma poured out into the air. The coffee smell was so intense, I wanted to take a sip of it myself. It was silent, around 9pm or so. My brother was upstairs in his room most likely talking to another friend that none of us knew about while Nur was playing quietly upstairs in our mother's room. Yuma just stared at me then, her eyes devoid of life, blinking back a fresh coat of tears. My heart ached instantly and I regretted sounding as harsh as I did--I didn't mean to hurt her, but I wanted her to see the reality of the situation. He never loved her, he was purely selfish for keeping our mother chained to an unloving relationship for over twenty years. It was cruel.

"Why am I not enough Amani? I love your father, I do everything for him. I just want him to love me."

"Why? He's ugly, inside and out. Be glad that you got rid of him," I joked trying to lighten the air. She sighed before taking a sip of her coffee. The summer night was warm, and the streets were quiet; the clock ticked ever so softly but bounced off the walls to disturb the peace between my mother and I. Nights like this depressed me. The house retired by 10pm and there was nothing left for a college student like myself to do when I was so accustomed to being in bed by 2am. I looked at my mother, and yet again my heart ached for her. I don't think it's possible for anyone to love their mother as much as Ilham and I do--our love for her was fierce and unwavering. We'd sacrifice our lives for her, and I know many kids say that, but the culture that the Palestinians of the Syracuse Community created wasn't friendly or safe. Our relatives were like the mafia, horrible beings you didn't want to cross paths with--our small family being the exception to that--we were good and honest people who were just trying to get by.

I got up and sat next to my mother giving her a hug; I didn't know how to help her feel better. Anything I ever said went right in one ear and out the other, but I still needed to try.

"Yuma, you're a beautiful woman, I guarantee you that his new girlfriend isn't nearly as pretty as you. She's probably with him because he's spending money he doesn't have with other people's credit cards. Women are disgusting like that sometimes."

"He's got a good family; all his kids are good and you and Ilham are in college. He's got a great wife who cooks and cleans! Any man would want that, right?"

She looked at me then, eyes filled with so much sadness that they pleaded silently, saying, "hey I tried keeping the tears at bay, but failed". It pained me to see her so sad, she was such a small, fragile woman and to see her this upset made me angry with my dad. *Why did he have to hurt such a good woman? Sure she was a bit overwhelming at times but who isn't?* It wasn't fair to her--Not fair at all. So I hugged her again as she cried. It was all I could do for her at the moment.

Love often confused me. *Why were those who gave every bit of themselves in a relationship taken advantage of? Where is the harm in returning the love if you feel it? Why is there this stigma attached to a man or woman's ego that prevents them from delving into loving someone, full heartedly. Why was it such a crime?*

"Aww Yuma, don't cry. Some men subconsciously feel like they don't deserve the good things in their life, so they act up or leave to confirm, making it so that they were never good enough to begin with. It's weird I know, there's not much logic behind the things people do. Seeking to understand such things will lead you further down this road of confusion you're already on."

I believe the saddest sound in the world is the crashing waves of your mother's tears flowing down the forefront of her perfect face. For never have I heard a cry with so much pain as Yuma's tonight. She asked me *why* for many more nights after that, always turning to me for the answer her eyes begged me to give. I failed her in those moments because the sad truth to it is that I wasn't screwed up like Alzalim. I had a heart unlike his, a heart that beats, that felt love in its truest form, that breathed compassion and sympathy. My veins pumped passion and emotions into my body to supply me with the necessary feelings of what was required as a decent human being. There was no way I could comprehend and then describe the heart of a man who didn't love himself to begin with, much like you couldn't ask God to understand the ways of the devil...you could only ask the Demon himself.

CHAPTER 9

Poisoned with Depression

"There is no life to be found in violence. Every act of violence
brings us closer to death. Whether it's the mundane violence
we do to our bodies by overeating toxic food or drink or the
extreme violence of child abuse, domestic abuse, domestic
warfare, life-threatening poverty, addiction, or state terrorism."

- Bell Hooks

The gripping reality of any situation involving another individual is that you can never be one hundred percent sure of what's going on in their heads, why, and how it causes them to react to any given situation. Let's say there is always that point one percent chance that you will never know and there will never be a way you can find out; we can only make an estimated guess as to why things happen and the reasoning behind the cause and effects they leave in their wake. I believe the same thing happened in the case of Yuma. As a child growing up, I never understood many, if not all, of the emotions she was going through because I was too young to digest and analyze the events that caused the onslaught of terrible memories I have as a child growing up. Poison. I felt she was poisoned.

The beginning of the memory is a tad bit fuzzy but it clears up during the moments where it matters most. The night was young, the moon shone bright and white in the calm blanket of stars covering our city on this night. The air was warm and sweet, carrying an aura of stress- free vibes. It started off as any other night would in any of the calm and quiet house-holds lining Elm Street. That night, two of our cousins were spending the night which carried immense excitement for the three of us, given we were never allowed guests as children. So, it was a pretty big deal to us.

The Nintendo 64 was all set up with Mario Kart 64 in its slot ready to be played by us all. Just at that moment, lights flashed through the windows alerting us that a car had come by. Excited with anticipation, we ran to the window as fast as we could and peered behind the curtain onto the street where a car stood parked, engine running.

The door opened and out came both our cousins: the boy named Malik, and the other, a girl named Farah. Their mother waved to us when she spotted the three of us, faces pressed against the warm glass. Smiling, we waved back and motioned for our cousins to hurry in and so, they ran in. The air was filled with giggling and cheer as we brought them over to our room and sat them down to begin playing the game. The sparks of competition flew high, our palms and thumbs ready to throw turtle shells and speed away in flashing rainbow colors to the finish line. All of a sud-den, Ilham, opening her Pepsi too quickly, caused it to overflow and spill onto the red carpet that covered our apartment.

"Oooooooo," we simultaneously chimed as we watched the soda bub-ble go down into a massive brown puddle on the carpet.

"Shhh!" Ilham warned us, "I don't want Yuma to hear and get myself in trouble, so please be quiet." We all stood quietly and watched for what

would happen next, hoping the soda would just dry up on its own--but it wouldn't.

Panicked, Ilham ran out of the room and returned minutes later with a hand towel, which she dropped on the soda spill and sat right on top of it. Believing the situation had been resolved, we all turned our attention back to the screen and started the video game. Ten minutes into the race, Yuma came walking in to check on us, to make sure things were running as smoothly as possible for the sleepover. She scanned the room, and in doing so, noticed that Ilham was sitting on a hand towel.

"What are you sitting on Ilham?" she asked, curious.

Shaking her head, Ilham responded, "Nothing Yuma, just a shirt."

"Really? Get up."

"Huh?"

"I said get up," Yuma scolded, angrier this time. Once Ilham rose from her position on the towel, she exposed the part where the Pepsi had leaked. Yuma walked over to her spot and bent down to examine the spill. Once she analyzed the spill and concluded it was in fact soda, she turned to Ilham and smacked her clean across the face. The sound hurt my ears badly; her hand resembled a whip the way it spun so fast across Ilham's cheek, leaving a visible mark, in its wake.

We all stood there shocked, paralyzed by the bluntness of the incident, with fear gripping the air we breathed. The game played on in the background, it's playful and catchy tune trying to entice us back. But our attention was turned to Ilham's inflamed cheek. She cradled it with the palm of her hand and cowered away in defense. But Yuma's wrath didn't end there; next, she grabbed a fistful of Ilham's thick and voluminous hair, yanking so hard that she nearly pulled Ilham off the ground and into her. Without releasing her grip, she dragged Ilham past the living room and her bedroom, until both of them entered the salown, where Ilham's tears and wails echoed into the room we were occupying. Goosebumps rose atop my skin; the fear of her cries filled and paralyzed us to our core.

The sound of Ilham's cries, as she begged for Yuma to stop, carried over loudly as if they floated through the walls and engulfed us with the sound of her pain. "Yuuuuuuuuummmmaaaaa, please--please stop--ooowwww!!!" she wailed, choking on her tears.

To hear Ilham cry out in such pain terrified me; the sound of someone being broken and humiliated did a number on you. Witnessing such violence made you mature in ways you shouldn't have to at such a young age. It made you realize that even though we were her children, even though we were too young to comprehend the consequences of our mistakes, we faced punishments over them.

I slowly crept out of the tv room and got into a crawling position to peer into the next room. I was able to see past the room and into the sala where the incident was happening. Ilham's hair was being torn from her head and thrown into the air--the dark room seemed ever more chilling by witnessing the abuse. I caught a look at Ilham's face as she pleaded and begged...her face was soaked in tears and trauma. I couldn't look away--I tried but I couldn't-- something in me told me that this moment needed to be witnessed.

Yuma's face scared me; she didn't look satisfied. She continued on and on, beating and ripping through Ilham's hair. The particles being torn from her scalp made me cringe and caress my own head of hair. Tears welled up in my eyes seeing Ilham's pain; how much hair did Yuma need to pull to be content with her punishment? What was this doing for her? What was it accomplishing? I've never seen such a look on Yuma's face--little did we know this event would set the pace for what the rest of our childhood would look like.

Ilham finally broke free from Yuma's grasp and wailed and cried on her way back to the tv room. She sat in the corner, knees to chest, face *covered and buried in her thighs. My cousins, Ayman and I looked at her shaking body which made us nervous and anxious ourselves. Our cousins looked terrified, more so than I'd expected; they ran out of the room, demanding to call home and ask to be taken back. Yuma complied, not saying anything to them as we all waited silently for their ride to pull up and take them back to their safe haven.*

I watched sadly as their car pulled off and began to understand that they would never want to come back. I understood that we'd never have the chance to have a sleepover, not if something like this would happen again.

Turning my attention back to Ilham, I slowly approached her, "Hey, are you okay?"

Yea, it was a dumb question, but it was all I could offer at the moment and I wanted to give her any comfort I could. I felt useless and tried to hide the fact that I was shaking in fear. Ilham slowly lifted her head--her appearance made me gulp hard and I tried not to grimace at the look of her. She was a mess--her face beaten red with scratches all over and, blood dripped from her head. Her hair looked atrocious; it was knotted and torn, while her scalp seemed red like she could have been skinned. But her face...her face is what pulled at my heartstrings. She looked so defeated, so traumatized and scared; what more could I offer her than my tears? Her green eyes were filled with oceans over, her glassy, glossy eyes; it broke my heart. Ilham looked like an abused puppy, her eyes asking all the questions her tongue couldn't utter due to the shock.

I shook my head and hugged her, crying and telling her that everything would be okay. Things would be fine eventually, and it will all be forgotten one day.

I sat staring at Yuma while she sipped her coffee beside me on the couch. The memory wasn't forgotten, nor did I want to forget it. As I grew older and wiser that memory served as evidence of the day her poison set in and took root in her soul. It affected the way she nurtured, the way she behaved, and the way she respected herself. It was the start of the long battle that would consume her, bring her to her knees and break her spirit.

This poison, that crept its way through her open wounds, disguised its presence until it broke into the chambers of her heart and the control center within her mind. It was unwelcomed and unannounced as it gripped her and chained her down to its call and command. She was a slave to its needs and desires, wanting company alongside her misery; it caused her to do unmotherly deeds. Knowing that it was a force to be reckoned with, knowing that it was incurable once fully accepted as it was within her body and ready for action.

The battle beginning long ago when I was too young and uninformed, had been temporarily lost, but I was older and wiser now. The war was now ours, and this poison would be expelled from within her soon enough, our scars served as a reminder of what mission we were on. Often times I sat wondering why Ilham and I fought for Yuma so hard when our entire lives were spent being abused by her. Alzalim didn't lay his hands on us nearly as much as she did given he was imprisoned most of our lives and yet we still chose her side over his.

The sound of her sipping silently in the emptiness of her environment made it clear then, she was alone. Even though Khalto was now living in America, she was a woman too which meant she couldn't really come to Yuma's defense or put others in their place for her. Had her brother been here I'm sure situations would be different but he wasn't and they weren't. Yuma was consistently oppressed by her husband's family with no support as her backbone. She needed us more and more as we grew older, and with the years gone by we understood why she inflicted pain on us. The scars she left my siblings and I seared into our memories, keeping track of the poison within her, waiting for our chance to rid ourselves of it …even if the poison was depression.

CHAPTER 10

A Visit to Graves St.

"There is no detachment where there is no pain.
And there is no pain endured without hatred or
lying unless detachment is present too."

– Simone Weil

There are those rare moments that stop your heart, moments where time stands still and the world goes silent. All you hear is the shallow breathing of your lungs taking in air as you stand there, still and shocked. You wonder if this will be the moment that stops your heart for good, or if you'll walk away breathing for another day.

Moments like these were hell...

Moments like these...my dad caused...

"Hello?" my dad's deep but annoying voice called out as it shattered its way into my thoughts.

He just stopped by unexpectedly, dropping in to say hi after being back in Syracuse for a week. I was relieved he was finally getting it over with, so he could get the hell out and live his life separately from our own.

We all stood there staring at him, not knowing what to say, because none of us cared that he was back. Even Nur, who was now 6, wasn't comfortable being near him (which sucked for him because he always used Nur as a scapegoat whenever he didn't want to talk to anyone in the family). Now, she was no longer willing to jump into his arms happily; the man had abandoned her for over a year! *Did you really think she wouldn't catch onto the fact that you left her? That's pathetic, even for you.*

Ayman was the first to speak, walking painfully to Yaba before giving him an awkward hug.

"Hey Alzalim, so you're back huh?" He made small talk as if our father had been out researching a cure to cancer or building houses in Africa. *The man was in jail for petty crimes Ayman! Save your breath for someone that matters.*

"Yea, until court," he answered shortly. He didn't want to be here--we all knew that--but he had to come so that he could tell the rest of the Palestinian community that he came over, and that WE were the ones that didn't want him around. That was true, we didn't want him around, but he needed to stop using us as an excuse to claim his freedom. He had already proven that what he wanted was a life without strings holding him down--a life without a wife to come home to and a family to kiss good night. Why didn't he claim that lifestyle and explain his reasoning for living the life he was living? If we really hadn't wanted him around, we would have left him for dead a while ago when he was back in prison. *I really hate my father, I really do.*

"Come here," my father demanded without any emotion whatsoever. I made eye contact with him then. My skin flushed with goosebumps and my heart beat steadily increased; this man's eyes looked like death--they were fierce, with no sign of love or compassion. His eyes, they looked like the eyes of a murderer. He wrapped his arm around my shoulder then, placed a kiss on my cheek, and asked how I was doing.

Being scared out of my wits, I started vomiting words out, saying anything irrelevant or esoteric that he wouldn't understand. "So I'm applying for an internship opportunity with a psychologist here in 'cuse! I'll get to see what it's like on the inside--get to help diagnose conditions and compare theories with one another to see if there's a correlation with the patient's condition and their past history with--"

"Yea, yea, that's great to hear, you're doing good things. Where's Ilham?" he quickly interrupted. I wanted to smirk knowing that he didn't understand a word that was coming from my mouth, but bit my lip to keep from laughing.

"She's not here, she's an RA for the summer again," I informed him. He nodded his head slowly before noticing Nur wasn't there.

"Nur!" he called into the vast openness upstairs. There was no response. "Nur!" he called again. The small trotting of feet was heard before Nur appeared at the top of the stairs. Looking down she saw her father and her smile was wiped clean from her face. She stood there then, just staring at our dad with a far-away look in her eyes. You could tell she didn't know what to say or do; she hadn't seen him in over a year, so she wasn't comfortable enough with him to go running after him.

Children are different than adults in that way--when someone is missing for a long period, they completely wipe that person's existence from their mind. They can't really comprehend a loved one leaving in that way; they can't wrap their heads around the fact that their loved one didn't want them. So, they just simply erase the person from their minds. He wasn't supposed to exist, yet here he was before her and she had no clue how to act.

"Come here Yaba, come say hi," he said to her. In our culture, parents call their children "Yaba", "Baba", "Momma", or "Yuma" to reciprocate their affection. Nur didn't budge; instead, she looked at me as I looked back. I smiled, my way of encouraging her to just get it over with so he could leave, but she didn't budge.

"Nur come here," he ordered once more, this time a little agitated. Again, she didn't move. It was only then that I realized that my aunt, Sakina, who came to visit from Palestine was right next to him (the aunt with the 8-9 kids). She laughed and asked Nur to come to her, to which Nur responded by walking down the steps ever so slowly to her side.

"Go say hi to Alzalim, he missed you," she cooed to her. Nur looked at her with an awkward smile before fidgeting her feet and hiding her face in Sakina's shirt. Our dad stood there for a moment, his fake smile wiped clean from his face, replaced by an annoyed frown. This time around he didn't need us the way he used to when he was in prison, so that pathetically artificial smile wasn't there.

He sighed with annoyance, clearly not wanting to be here. We didn't want him here either. Sakina exchanged a few words with us while my dad slowly edged his way out of the house and onto the sidewalk where the sun blazed hotly in the sky. Things were different now; before he'd pretended to care, now he just couldn't give two craps. It wasn't like I cared, but still....*put on a show for Nur, her of all people need it.*

Once my father and aunt left, I took my seat on the couch and just thought about how life would be knowing he was in the city but not in our lives. It sounded too good to be true, honestly because there's no way he'd live in the city without wanting to bother the hell out of us. The thing about him is that he thrived off of hurting others, ruining people's reputations or his own children's reputations. He loved the rush of adrenaline that came with it--that sense of power and the hopelessness he'd put the family through.

It was a throne he'd tear others down for....a throne I aimed to dismantle.

CHAPTER 11

Suicide's Punch Card

"We can consciously end our life almost anytime we choose.
This ability is an endowment, like laughing and blushing,
given to no other animal…in any given moment, by not
exercising the option of suicide, we are choosing to live."

– Peter McWilliams

I f you knew that someone wanted to commit suicide or had planned
on committing suicide, what would you do? What about after the
fact? Say that whomever you knew failed at their attempt or, God forbid,
they were able to put out the flicker of light in their soul. What thoughts
would consume you? Would you feel sadness in knowing that you were
probably one of the last few who witnessed them alive and about? Or
anger maybe, at the fact that they felt that suicide was their only way out
of whatever it was that was ailing them? A list of emotions comes to my
mind among many: Shock, disbelief, sorrow, fear, hesitation, anger, disappointment, and confusion. My thoughts regarding such a hypotheti-
cal event overwhelm me, leaving little to no room for comprehension.

I know what contemplating the choice of suicide feels like, as I've experienced it many times over the span of my young life. For example, while facing my own irrational obsession with bulimia, retching so hard that blood would spill out, questioning my reflection and lack of self-love--I often wondered if living was even worth it. During those moments, I knew how welcoming the thought of suicide felt, disguised in the idea that all you had to do was feel one last sharp pang of pain that would end it all--the idea that nothing else would hurt you or hang over you like a leech consuming your life force. I didn't think about my loved ones, didn't think about my friends, didn't think about all the chance meetings I would have in the future helping others through their issues and making a difference in others' lives. No, during those times, all I could think about was the dark abyss I found myself in and the promise of being left alone, forever floating in a land inhabited only by those who thought to cut God's plan short. I had never quite understood what the other side felt like, the side of those receiving the news of their loved one committing or attempting suicide. I would come to learn that it was a scary reality.

It was a rare occurrence, in which we all spent an afternoon together watching TV in the living room. Normally, this never happened, given Ilham was always working and Ayman was trapped in his room playing games online. It was an afternoon in which we all enjoyed each other's company; I tried my best to capture the image in my head to recall it in the future when things wouldn't be this good or peaceful.

Just then, Yuma came in and sat beside Ilham watching the scene play about for a bit,

"Make sure you guys always look out for each other okay? Remember that even though you guys don't have the most perfect relationship, all you have is each other, so always...always...always defend one another, okay?"

Her voice was so soft and calm; she seemed tired. We all turned our attention to her while Nur ran up to her and hugged her knees. Yuma gave a slight smile before picking Nur up and kissing her hard on the cheek.

"I love you guys, you know."

"We love you too Yuma, so much" we simultaneously answered. Seeing her fragile figure made me want to scoop her up and cradle her. She carried such sorrow in her steps, in which there was no will--no excitement. It made me angry that we couldn't do anything to change that.

She pulled from within the pocket of her bra a wad of bills. Handing us each a couple hundred dollars, we all looked at one another confused.

"And this is for?" Ilham asked for us all.

"For you guys, I feel bad that you guys never get what you want. Make sure to spend it wisely and never forget what I told you guys. Always be there for one another and try never to fight please, okay?"

"Okay Yuma."

"I'm going to sleep. I'm tired." Once again, we all told her we loved her as she slowly climbed up the steps in her Tinkerbell pajamas. Her hair was pulled into a ponytail, with a few loose strands making their way in front of her face. It was evident how tired she was; she didn't look like she could make it up the stairs without help.

I stared at the bills in my hand, noting that this was unlike her to give us this much money. Four hundred each? That was a bit too much, even for Yuma. She was very meticulous about how she allocated money since we didn't have any. I decided I would save it, and that when she woke up I'd just give it back to her, because I was sure she'd need it more than I did.

A few hours later Ilham looked around before asking, "Did anyone notice Yuma come down yet?"

Ayman and I exchanged looks, "No we didn't."

Getting up, I let them know that I'd check on her; I was beginning to sense that they both were just as suspicious about the money as I was. Heading upstairs, I knocked on her door but there was no answer. I knocked again and still, no answer. Jiggling the door knob, I noted the door was locked which was unusual because she always kept it unlocked, unless Alzalim was here. He always locked the door.

"Yuma," I called into the crevice of the door. "Yuma, open the door."

There was no answer.

I banged on the door, "Yuma, open the door."

Still no answer.

"YUMA, OPEN THE DOOR!" I screamed louder, banging with more force. I began to freak out and my anxiety skyrocketed. "Please God, please don't tell me my suspicions were correct, please God," I pleaded as I slammed my body on the door, putting all my weight down on it.

"Please, open the door Yuma, please!" I screamed.

I slammed my body into the wood once more putting every bit of strength and effort into slamming this piece of crap door. I felt the pressure of the door release as the lock busted open, and I came flying into her room. That's when I saw it--the empty bottle of pills--fear gripped my core, causing me to immediately hold my breath. Running over to Yuma, I checked for any signs of breathing.

Her breath was there but very faint; tears welled up in my eyes quicker than I knew what to do with.

"You're so stupid Amani, you knew something was up; you should've checked on her sooner!" I cried to myself, shaking her.

Tears rushed in waves as they dropped down on Yuma's body while, with futile rescue aids, I attempted to revive her.

"Yuma please, please, please wake up, please wake up!" I screamed. My nostrils were soaked in tears, my vision growing blurrier as I slapped Yuma over and over again.

"ILHAM HELP!!! YUMA TRIED KILLING HERSELF!!! SHE WON'T WAKE UP PLEASE!!!"

I heard rushing as Ilham raced up the stairs to meet me. She carried the same expression of self-loathing as I did. I knew she was insulting herself too from the looks of it.

"We need to wake her up!" she ordered.

Once again, I shook Yuma one last time before slapping her as hard as I could but it wouldn't work. Clasping my hands together tightly I placed them on her chest and began pumping as I counted in my head. Ilham called out to Yuma as she slapped her. It was then that, by some miracle, Yuma woke up.

"Go and throw up right now!!!" Ilham ordered. Yuma said nothing as she grabbed her glass and slowly walked into the bathroom, beginning the process of throwing up the pills she had forced upon herself. Once she finished we needed to get her to a hospital for screenings to be sure she would be fine.

I sat, huddled in a ball, terrified at what just happened...at what I had encountered. My mind raced through all the events that had occurred earlier in the day with Yuma in the living room.

Was that it? Was that all she really wanted to say to us as her last words?

"You're a coward Yuma!! You hear me! You're a coward!! You have a baby girl!! If not for us, then live for her!!!" I cried sobbing without control. I was angry as was Ilham who stood there with more control, yet she also looked peeved.

Was that really how she planned on leaving us? With a few hundred bucks and no parental figures? We weren't old enough to care for an entire family. Hell, I wasn't even twenty-one yet! We were all suffering and enduring life when all it gave us was sorrow, yet we weren't offing ourselves! I was so livid, all I could see was red: "How could you even think *of leaving us behind!! You birthed us!! You are our mother and no matter how rough things get we all have each other; what made you forget that, huh?!"*

I looked to Ilham before grabbing her leg and sobbing into her knee; she dropped down to hug me then. I felt her shaking. What does a warrior do when the queen they serve kills herself? Does that make it Ilham's mission to protect us or does her new task involve raising us for Yuma's sake?

It was all too much to bear, and poor Nur had no idea of these turn of events. So innocent, so young, already without the love of her father, and here Yuma was trying to escape this world and leave her without a mother too? It was absurd, Yuma couldn't quit. This is her job; she needed to stick around until the end. It was her duty as a parent to be there and step up even when times were at their worst.

I was scared, but what terrified me more was the knowledge that this incident was not her only suicide attempt. According to Yuma, she tried two more times after that, without us around, so that she could try and successfully take her life. Saying she didn't want to live anymore because she was tired of the stress and pressure being placed on her from our relatives. No matter how good of a wife she was, there was always something they blamed her for and never him. "But," she confided, "for some reason God saved me in both circumstances. I don't know why he kept me around to continue living in this hell, but maybe it's because one of you will one day be worth my while and actually make me proud."

Finding out this new bit of information led me to see her in such a different light; it led me to ask myself questions I didn't want to know the answers to. To know that at times, unbeknownst to any of us, Yuma was out in the world attempting suicide and she could have possibly succeeded, terrified me. How would that news have been delivered? Who would deliver it? How would we take it after witnessing, first-hand, her second attempt? Should we have reported her to a suicide hotline? Wouldn't they have deemed her an unfit mother and taken her from us? There were far too many questions, too many scenarios that I didn't want to face if they meant that she'd be there at the start and not at the end. She was our mother, through thick and thin, we were a family, and a life without her felt like death itself.

CHAPTER 12

Unresolved Terror

"The purpose of terror lies not just in the violent act itself. It is in producing terror, it sets out to enflame, to divide, to produce consequences, which they then use to justify further terror."

– Tony Blair

What does someone hope to gain from instilling fear in others? Respect? Submission? Affection? Companionship? Loyalty? Or is it just an ego trip, knowing that people cower in your presence, that in your wake you create silence and oppression?

Those types of individuals gain nothing but the prayers from those who've been wronged, to stumble upon the throne created from such acts of violence, and die a slow and enlightened death. Liberation and freedom will inspire an uprising--all it takes is for one person to rebel. It just takes one person to realize that they are human and vulnerable. Not a God, but quite simply a human being. And once that is fully acknowledged, you will not be able to stop a person who is determined to gain control of their life...of their future. That kind of determination will ignite a fire within them so strong that nothing and no one can stop it.

Alzalim embodied that imbalance of power to me. He exuded such an aura of fear and intimidation that I lost all confidence and bravery, whenever he was around. He was able to suck the life from within me and able to make me cower in submission without raising a finger. His presence made itself known before he showed his face--the mere vibrations of his existence seeping through crevices and cracks, with the thought of him, creating a black cloud where there was once sunshine. I was ashamed of myself every time he succeeded in making me cower. He didn't deserve my fear...he didn't deserve my submission. And yet, in his presence, I never failed to play my role as the terrified, little kid playing in his long and terrible reign. I could never understand what it was about this man that terrified me so...why he was able to create such a feeling within me and not even know it. It was the main reason why I could not stand him.

There was a time two years ago in high school when I had an innocent crush on a boy in my school who I only saw during my lunch period. He was always making me laugh; humor was something that could allow anyone to catch my attention. I enjoyed smiling and laughing whenever I could because I knew that once I got home, I wouldn't be enjoying myself or have any great company. But Daniel made me laugh, made me smile, and what made me happiest was that he didn't see me as a 'towelhead' the way others liked to refer to my sister and I. He saw me for me and that was it; and for that he earned my respect and my friendship. Daniel was unlike the rest of the boys in the school who tugged and pulled at my headscarf, back then I wore a hijab. Since the 6th grade, when I first entered puberty, I was required to cover up because I was developing as a woman. It wasn't until I entered my freshman year in college that I decided to tell my parents that I would do as my sister before me did and remove my hijab. I explained that I felt I was only wearing it for them and not for God, which made my reasons wrong. And like Daniel, they accepted me for me.

Seeing him daily made me smile because I was guaranteed to laugh at something ridiculous that day; he didn't care that he made a fool of himself to make others laugh, and to me, that was the best kind of person there could be. The pair of us decided to hang out after school one day after being unable to link up during our lunch period, it was an innocent event. But that event would soon manifest a series of moments creating a memory that defined Alzalim for me to this very day.

The school bell chimed signaling that classes were over and dismissal was underway. There was the usual clamor of students rushing to their lockers, making plans with one another and running to exit the building. The electricity in the air as everyone prepared for the weekend was intoxicating, and although I knew I had nothing planned, it was impossible not to catch the excitement in the air.

Waiting by the entrance to the school I scanned the influx of cars rolling in to see if Alzalim had arrived yet. As I peered into the parking lot I noticed his green Tahoe across the street by the stop sign staring coldly at me. Catching his icy gaze, my blood froze and I couldn't help but feel a gut instinct begging me to run inside and find another ride home. Placing my hand on my stomach, I ignored my reflex to run and pushed forward towards the direction of his truck. The closer I found myself to his car, the more terrified I felt; the urge to run grew stronger and stronger, and before I could change my mind I was at the passenger side of the truck, climbing in.

Buckling my seat belt I turned to Alzalim and forced a smile. "Hey thanks for picking me up," I said as cheerfully as I could.

He chewed the inside of his cheek for a bit before slowly nodding his head. "Who's Daniel?" he asked.

My heart tripped over its own beat. Swallowing, I stammered, "What do you mean?"

"Which one of these kids is Daniel?" he asked feigning a calm demeanor as his finger scanned the crowd of teens streaming out of the building.

I bit my lip, my body heat rising ten degrees hotter than I needed it to be. I could feel sweat starting to form throughout my body near his presence and I wanted nothing more than to just fade away. I prayed internally that this interrogation would just go away, that none of it would continue but he was waiting on a response. If I kept him waiting it would only anger him further. So I did what I thought was best in the moment and remained quiet. I was in trouble regardless of whether or not I said anything, so answering wouldn't save me from the fate that was already handed to me.

Sitting with Alzalim was torture. I waited until Ilham and Ayman approached the vehicle and gave Ilham a distressed look. She immediately caught my eye and gave a slight nod. My palms were sweating and my skin was slick with moisture; I was a nervous wreck and begged God to help me. Swearing to Him that if He got me out of this situation I would never look at Daniel again.

"Answer me!" Alzalim yelled angrily this time, not able to control his temper. I whimpered in my seat and shook my head. I wasn't going to give him any more reason to hurt me than he already had. He stared at me with his cold eyes, there was no humanity in them, no kindness or reason. He carried nothing in them but pure death and hatred; I could never understand what he hated so much--was it himself? Was it his actions that brought him to this very day? I had no clue, but this man wasn't one I called father by choice. He meant nothing to me; in fact, I hated him just as much as he hated himself.

"Okay you're not going to get anything from her, so there's no point in yelling at her like that!" Ilham cut in to my defense.

Alzalim turned to look at her with his cold stare and grimace aimed at her. But she did not shudder from his look; instead, she met it head on with a fierce look of her own. Ever the defender of the weak--ever the warrior--she had my envy and admiration. She never failed to impress me with her courage. In my eyes, she symbolizes freedom, for women like her could never be chained down and forced to submit to anyone's will.

"Wait until we get home, I'll check your Facebook; I know you've been speaking with him through there!" He retorted angrily as he shifted the car into drive and zoomed ahead without warning, causing us all to hit our seats hard. The car lurched through the streets without any consideration of any others in sight. He drove like a maniac normally, but today he was angry and that was evident.

Once we arrived home, Alzalim got out of the car and stepped into the house angrily. He yelled into the distance and his roar was heard through-out the street. Ayman jumped out of the car and entered the house. Just as I expected, he went straight into his room to ignore whatever was going to happen like he always did. Ilham tapped my shoulder, "Amani, I texted Sailani and told her to log into your Facebook and delete anything that could get you into trouble that has to do with Daniel. What's your email and password?" I looked to her then and I knew she could see it then; I knew she could see the fear in my eyes, the look of gratitude for having a sister like her. She was our protector and she knew it. It's as if she took on that role as we grew older, becoming our guardian angel in more ways than one. She saw how I hated myself for being afraid of him; she saw how I wanted to follow her courageous lead and be able to stand against him on my own one day--to stare evil in the face. I wanted to measure up to him--wanted him to see the fire within me--wanted him to see that he was not in control of my fate and that a man like him didn't deserve children like us in his life. He deserved children who gave him hell; we were too good for him.

"Amani!" Ilham shook me out of my reverie and I quickly gave her the information she needed. The rest was up to Sailani, I prayed she was as fast at deleting things as she was at texting me back. I felt blessed to have a friend like her in my life; not many could understand the life Ilham and I lived...and although she didn't fully understand it, she understood enough. She was someone I was thankful to have met, carrying a light I needed to look ahead and remind me that I had a future--one that was unwritten until I was ready to write it.

"Ilham, I'm scared; I don't want to go in there," I whimpered as tears welled in my eyes.

Nothing like this had ever happened in the family before; we'd always followed the rules and had never brought such anger to our parents. I was confused and didn't understand how having Daniel as a friend was cause for anger. I had done nothing with the boy; I just had an innocent crush on him. The drama over something so small was incomprehensible. My body couldn't stop shaking in fear, my breathing came in quick gasps, and yet my mind was operating separately from them. I couldn't fully wrap my head around what was happening and didn't really understand how serious the situation was. Nonetheless, I removed myself from Alzalim's car and slowly walked inside. Yuma came to me confused with a gaze filled with scrutiny.

"Amani shoo fee? (what's going on?)" she questioned. I met her look with a sad look of my own and shrugged my shoulders.

"Amani!!!" Alzalim bellowed from upstairs; I knew he was in our room for that was where the desktop was located. I sighed weakly and swallowed back tears that fought to be expelled from within me. Ilham gripped my hand in hers and whispered to me that she'd be right there with me. Ilham and I usually argued most of the time...well...all the time, but in the moments that we really needed one another, we never failed to be supportive. I felt that we were not conventional sisters, because the things we were forced to endure weren't what others had to.

Our childhood consisted of a depressed mother who beat and hurt us whenever her depression took control of her actions. Weekly prison visits marked our calendars in which we met kids of other felons. We made friends that we'd never see again and had grown up understanding the darker side of life. We were children who lived as if on fire, feeling the heat consume our lives, but letting others believe our lives were perfect.

I clung onto Ilham's hand as we entered our room seeing Alzalim's huge frame hunched over the small desktop. He thoroughly combed through my Facebook account, and to his disappointment, couldn't find anything to incriminate me. I made a mental note to thank Sailani for being so quick to help me out without asking questions. She was a God send.

Determined to find out who Daniel was, he went through my friends' list and searched for his name. Being that he was the only one who showed up once his name was fully typed into the search box, he clicked on it. Daniel's page popped up, and along with his profile, his number was attached to his information page. I sighed mentally; of course he'd have his number out there...idiot.

Grabbing the house phone, Alzalim dialed the number on the screen and waited. I lunged forward to try and stop him, but Ilham restrained me and told me not to do that. I shook my head and tears starting to pool down my face. "God, please don't let him do this!" I prayed silently.

Hearing the ringing continue, I hoped it would go to voicemail, but instead of my prayers being answered, Daniel picked up.

"Hello?" came his voice on the line; the poor kid was ignorant to all of this. He didn't deserve to be threatened by Alzalim.

"Yea, is this Daniel?" he asked with his false calm demeanor.

"Yes, who is this?" Daniel asked.

"I'm Amani's dad; I hear you two are flirting with one another. I see that you like baseball. Listen, if I EVER catch you near my daughter again...so much as look at her...I will break your knees with a baseball bat and see to it that your future is ruined. You got that?!" he yelled into the receiver. There was no response and instead the phone went dead. Hanging the phone up, Alzalim turned to me and towered over me, his gaze menacing and deadly.

"Don't ever let me catch you talking to that man again, you hear me?!" he yelled. Tears continued to stream down my face as I stared back at him, my lower lip quivering. I hated him. I hated him. I hated him. There was a better way to go about this than threatening the boy.

He grabbed a hold of my arm and squeezed tightly, "I didn't hear you!" he spit in my face.

"I think she understands what you're saying; God, you got spit all over her!" Ilham retorted, cutting in between us. He said nothing as they faced off in a stare. Leaving the room, I watched as Yuma came in and gave me a disapproving look. I looked away from her and climbed into bed, crying.

Ilham rubbed my back as I sat there feeling pathetic and weak. Eventually sleep caught up to me as my body was exhausted from all the fear it had experienced. The only place I could escape was to a world within my dreams. It was the only place where I could do as I pleased, make friends with who I wanted to, and laugh with Daniel as I so enjoyed doing. But dreams don't last forever, and once you've awakened, reality sets in as heavy and as dark as the night sky that peeked through my window. My pillow was damp from my tears; the room was dark and cold. I sat there staring into the darkness for God knows how long before Ilham came in and sat beside me.

"How are you feeling?" she asked. I didn't want to speak, so I shrugged my shoulders. She continued, "I have something I need to tell you, it's important."

I turned my head to look at her then; meeting her eyes, I saw she had trouble finding the right words. I continued to stare at her until she just blurted:"Ayman told Alzalim; apparently he was worried that you'd give your virginity to Daniel, so he snitched."

I suddenly found my voice then, "He did what?! That-that-ughhh!! Such a snitch, of course that's why he ran into his room like a coward!" I yelled angrily as I pounded on the neighboring wall that he and I shared.

"Coward!! Snitch!! Fraud!!" I yelled as I pounded on the wall. What a traitor! He'd sell any one of us if that meant getting in good with the father that didn't care about him or want him. I would pity him on another day, but today I felt rage over his betrayal. It was a day I would remember--a day that served as a reminder that he could not be trusted with secrets any longer.

Ilham grabbed my fists and urged me to settle down because Alzalim was in the next room watching TV. I didn't care then. I looked at her with unshed tears.

Ilham sighed and hugged me, "Yea, I know. I was shocked too, but what can we do now? What's done is done."

I pushed away from my sister, then jumped out of my bed, and fumed with a boiling rage as I entered Ayman's room. He was lying on his bed, playing his computer games. Once I entered his room, he looked up and met my livid gaze.

I wanted nothing more than to punch him dead in his face for being such a traitor.

"You're pathetic. You're a coward. You're such a fake brother. Don't ever come to me for help. Don't ever come to me for protection; don't ever talk to me. You're dead to me; you're a traitor, and I can't wait until the day he betrays your loyalty and trust, so you can see what an idiot you are."

"I did it to protect you," Ayman answered calmly as he looked back to his computer screen. He was two years younger than me and yet, he acted as if he was the eldest.

"Protect me?" I laughed, "From what? Laughing?!"

"I was afraid you'd...you know."

"Have sex with him?!! Are you an idiot! He was my friend and yea, I had an innocent crush on him, but I know better than to do anything that stupid, and ruin our reputation! As if I need you looking out for me! You're so stupid sometimes I wonder how you're related to us! You weren't worried; you found an excuse to finally cozy up to him, and hoped that by being a snitch you'd be in his good graces. Well here's the part you didn't think about: Who'd want a snitch in their corner? All it takes is the right price to sell you out, and then boom! You'd turn your back on him!"

"Amani stop; that's enough. It's done and over with now. Nothing you say will change anything," Ilham cut in. I turned my angry gaze to her, before I stomped out of the room into the hall. Alzalim was outside his room now, looking down the hall at us. I didn't care that I was making a scene; I didn't care that I was now looking dead into his eyes with all the hatred I felt for him. In that moment, I didn't care what happened to me.

"Put your coat on, we're going for a ride." he said.

"No," I responded, "I'm not going anywhere."

"Put your coat on. Now," he demanded, before heading downstairs. I sighed. So much for confidence. What more did he want from me? To show him where the kid lived? I had no idea where Daniel lived, and if I did, I still wouldn't show him. He'd scared the poor kid enough; Daniel didn't need to switch area codes because of this man being a lunatic.

I grabbed my coat and shuffled into my boots, heading downstairs and out the door. I jumped into the back seat of Alzalim's car.

"I want you up here," he ordered. Jumping out of the car, I mouthed, 'I want you up here,' in a mocking tone before sliding into the front seat *and slamming the door closed. He said nothing as he started the car and revved it up with the heat blasting. Winters here were brutal and it often reached below zero temperature. So, it took a minute or two to get the car warmed and ready to go. The radio played softly in the background, with Ed Sheeran's 'I See Fire' floating throughout the car: "Oh misty eye of the mountain below, keep careful watch of my brothers' souls."*

Pulling out of the driveway, Alzalim said nothing as we went from one street to the next. A couple of streets over, we entered onto the highway ramp to which he pressed on the gas and joined the rest of the oncoming traffic.

"Do you understand why I do the things I do?" he asked.

I rolled my eyes, "If I understood I'd have snitched on myself long ago wouldn't I?"

"I do these things because I'm your father and I do what needs to be done to protect your innocence."

"Protect my innocence? What did you think was going to happen, huh? After a few laughs I'd jump into bed with him?"

"It's that simple."

"Yea, maybe for an American who lives a carefree life. But not for us, born Arab. Women like us carry the burden at such a young age to behave and act a certain way. You guys all expect us to be these little perfect samples of wives before we understand what that means. You groom us to become silent and obey orders as if we're lapdogs. We understand what our virginity means to the family; we understand what it means for our honor and reputation, so don't talk to me about upholding those values when you've slept with countless women. Ilham and I could be virgins to our deaths and we wouldn't be able to undo the dishonor you've brought to our last name." I crossed my arms and snuggled deeper into the seat mumbling, "I hate claiming your name."

"There are things you fail to understand, smart ass; and you won't understand them until you get older," he stepped on the gas harder now, going 10 mph above the recommended highway speed limit. I tightened my seatbelt, knowing he loved to race on the highway and paid no mind to what was going on ahead of us.

He continued with his rant, "Let me ask you something."

I sighed. Here we go. Whenever he said that phrase, it meant a useless rant was about to follow with no lesson behind it, because he'd jump from one subject to another and somehow it would end with something that was completely out of left field from the starting point..

Rolling my eyes, I answered, "What?"

"You continue to laugh and spend time with him, and then what? Huh? You think he's going to be happy with just making you laugh? He's going to want to kiss you one day and then touch you later on. He's going to end up wanting to be in bed with you and you won't know it until after the deed is done. That's how men think!"

"Let me ask YOU something; how stupid and naïve do you think I am? Huh? I was raised by a depressed woman who beat us, whenever she was in overwhelming pain over YOU. I was raised seeing the massive bag of pills, all shapes and sizes, that she thought she hid well from us. I heard how she cursed your name for leaving to these other states with other women, as she stayed home to raise us. I've seen how YOU tried to place blame on her for nothing at all--how YOU tried to find any reason to make your infidelities justified, when in truth, they never were. I KNOW how men think because I have YOU as a father; I've watched you play Yuma for years--watched how you scammed others with your sweet-talking manner. I've seen the worst at work, and for that reason, I will never be fooled by any man that ever lives."

"You're welcome. Don't you ever say I didn't teach you anything." He disgusted me; he truly disgusted me. How can he not feel any bit of guilt over causing this family so much pain and then turn around and act like he actually raised us to be this way.

"But there's one thing I want you to keep in mind always," he continued, as he pressed down harder on the gas. I was now starting to become worried, given he was going over way over the speed limit. He zoomed past the others on the highway and shifted lanes frequently to avoid the other cars. It was snowing heavily now, and I held onto the car door tighter, staring into the white horizon in fear. I couldn't see a thing! How could he see anything with his driving? The other cars were beeping angrily as he passed them by, with the snow breaking the stream of light that spewed from their headlights.

"Slow down!" I screamed. He didn't listen, as he sped up causing my body to mold into the car seat. With the speed and force of the car pushing me further down into my seat, I swallowed heavily and screamed once more for him to stop driving so recklessly.

We were going to die. The speedometer showed the arrow all the way to the right. I didn't want to see what speed we were at now, afraid that I'd go flying through the back window. I closed my eyes, convinced that today would be the day I died. I felt the hand of death touch my shoulder--it's prickly and icy fingers reaching my bones. My nerves that were previously causing my body to go on full alert mode, in a panicked frenzy, were now calm.

My body accepted the fate that would surely come. I felt numb to the world around me with the fire of the heater now growing cold, as it laced my skin with goosebumps. I pictured Nur's innocent face and beautiful smile that made me continue living another day in this wretched life I lived. I pictured Ilham's face, how brave and angelic she was in the face of danger. I thought of how grateful I was to have her at my side as my sister. I pictured Yuma's face, the woman I loved more than anything in the *world. I pictured her beautiful and fuzzy smile, however rare it was and hoped that I'd get to see it one day, even if it was in the afterlife.*

How does one accept a fate they aren't prepared for? How does one cope with the possibility of drawing their last breath? Maybe that's the thing with fate, the way it is unexpected. Maybe it is unexpected so that the impact is more powerful. Its influence reaches and spreads out to those around it, touching the souls of hundreds (if not thousands) and inspiring others to meet their fate and dare I say, challenge it.

Ed Sheeran continued to play his acoustic, his voice floating through the car, "And I see fire burn on and on.."

"I want you to remember that no matter what, if you ever do any-thing to bring dishonor to our family... I will kill you, and I will sit in jail happy knowing that you can no longer slut around bringing shame to our family's name."

What does someone hope to gain from instilling fear in others? Respect? Submission? Affection? Companionship? Loyalty? Or does the rush of power one feels, knowing they carry someone's life in their hands, distract them from self-assessment or reason. Does this over-whelming power distract them from seeing the monster they're creat-ing which brings anguish wherever they go. Unable to fool the demon inside, unable to escape the darkness within them that they've wel-comed in, they become prisoners of their own demons and succumb to hatred.

Alzalim placed the seed of pure terror within me that day--a terror so great it would lead me to break free from the chains he had bound me with in the past. The thing about terror is that, for it to work effec-tively, those subjected to it must fear it. But once it is challenged with courage...it becomes nothing.

CHAPTER 13

Happiness for a Dollar Plus Tax

"The richness of life lies in memories we have forgotten."

– Cesare Pavese

A few hours had passed since our father's visit. Once I finished thinking about every possible situation that could occur with him being here (and freaking myself out more than necessary), I headed upstairs to check on what Nur was doing.

As I climbed up the stairs, I heard Nur humming her *Frozen* tunes softly. I smiled and took a pause. I wanted to watch her play before interrupting her; she had an assortment of dolls beside her with play dough thrown about. If my mom were here she would flip, considering she was a clean freak. Nur carried such an innocent smile on her face--one as light as a feather. She carried the same dark circles that Ilham and her father carried which made her look tired, even though she was the liveliest of us all.

I can't explain it, but every time I looked at Nur my heart would hurt and I would feel overwhelmingly sad. She really didn't deserve this life; she deserved a family that oozed as much happiness as she does. This life, this setting, this family...she wasn't meant to live like this.

Nur looked up then and met my gaze with a smile so big you didn't understand how it could all fit on her face. She ran up to me and hugged me. Whenever she caught someone watching her she would run up to the individual and just hug them. It was her way of showing her love. I smiled as her little voice chimed, "I love you Amani". I patted her back and replied, "I love you too, Nur."

Nur detached herself from me and ran over to her toys. As she resumed her play and active imagination, I couldn't help but be overwhelmed by memories of my siblings and I when we were younger.

We were very poor when we were kids; our father was in prison and my poor mother was left trying to raise kids in a country she hardly knew, as well as, its native language. During most of those days, I remember her sleeping; depression weighed heavily on her then with a huge bag of pills recommended by her psychiatrist.

Back then, our house was really quiet. Without cable to watch paid channels (like Disney), we resorted to watching PBS Kids and waited patiently for shows like *Zoboomafoo* and *Dragon Tails* to come on the TV. Most of the time, there were reruns, but we didn't mind-- we were grateful.

Similar to Nur, we had active imaginations. Ilham, Ayman, and I would work feverishly on our next project. We couldn't afford to buy toys as kids, so we'd get construction paper from our elementary school and build our toys. Crazy, right? I know, but it was truly beautiful how in sync we were when it came time to build them. I can't help but smile as I think back to all three of us sitting in a circle, cutting, and pasting away as we created our toys. So giddy were we, with the thought of finishing up so that we could start playing, come nightfall.

To many, it would seem sad that children had to make their toys out of paper,--to say the least--but we didn't notice that fact. We were lonely kids spending time with one another and our imaginations went wild. There wasn't much to do, so we worked with what we had. Paper just happened to be an item that was easily accessible for kids attending elementary school. Coloring and pasting was half the grade.

A memory I can clearly remember was when we grabbed two of our kitchen chairs, planted them side by side, and covered them in paper to make an ice cream truck. We then colored blank paper red, blue, and green on both sides crumpled them up, and placed them on top of cone shaped paper to make an ice-e. It's such a fond memory due to the fact that we worked so hard and so long on the project. Why, the truck practically took us half the day! But when we were finished--oh man, I swear we walked around like our truck was the best darn truck the city had to offer. We sang ice cream truck tunes loud and proud, as we pretended to put in our orders and lick our artificially made ices.

During these days, my mom would tell us, "Now I'm going to sleep. If you guys are good and quiet when I'm asleep, we'll go to the dollar store and you can each get ONE thing and ONE thing only".

Our hearts would soar so high.. One toy?! That meant the world to us, considering how poor we were. The occasions were rare, but when they arrived, nothing seemed more exciting! We paused our ice cream truck adventure, and looked on over to our mother as she lay asleep in her bed. We were eager to have her awaken and take us to the land of toys, but she seemed to sleep forever.

Time ticked ever so slowly in our small apartment. The world seemed quiet and the days dragged on. We didn't get to play outside often, due to the fact that my mom would have to watch us and during the dark, winter days, she was almost always in bed. We sighed, thinking that our mother would probably sleep the day away, but 20 minutes later, she woke up and got dressed. The smell of her perfume floated past our nostrils, alerting us that Yuma was leaving the house. We knew that whenever she had on her expensive perfume, we were all going to head out somewhere.

We smiled so hard that day, getting up so quickly and rushing to put our shoes on that we toppled over one another. I don't know why, but for some reason this memory of that day seemed to be one of my favorite childhood memories. I just can't explain it.

When we pulled into the Dollar Tree parking lot, we all rushed out of the car and ran inside, despite Yuma's order to stay by her side. Can you blame us? This was one of the few times as kids that we felt normal and a part of the crowd.

"Welcome to Dollar Tree!" called the employee by the door as we rushed past her. Our sights were on one thing and one thing only, in aisle one, the land of toys. We scoured through the lane, inspecting every item to see which toys would last long and which wouldn't. When we were unsure of which toy would last, we'd hold it up, call out Ilham's name, and ask for her verdict.

"No, that's gonna break," she'd say, for instance. If so, we received the message, drop the toy and scurry off to find another. At the end of our dollar tree frenzy, my sister and I ended up with teddy bears (Ilham's was burgundy and mine was grey). She named her bear Melina and I named mine Amanda; my brother on the other hand, purchased toy soldiers that came in a pack of 30 or so.

"Wanna play with me Amani?" Ayman asked with his wide smile, the excitement written all over his face.

"Yea," I responded. He was our only brother and I knew he needed someone to play with, so why not be the tomboy sister he needed for now?

"Have a nice day!" the cashier said, as she finished our transaction.

All three of us smiled at her, "Thank you!" We scurried off then, trailing behind our mother, getting into the car, and beginning our trip back home. In those moments, I knew my mother was happy that she managed to put a smile on our faces, even though she didn't smile then...I knew she was happy.

CHAPTER 14

Clinging onto Silence

"Silence is the sleep that nourishes wisdom."

– Francis Bacon

This morning felt like the mornings before my father's arrival back home. I'd wake up in bed, staring up at the ceiling, just listening. What for? Anything really; my body would be booting up as I just sat there thinking and listening to the world going on around me.

Summer days dragged on in our household. Yuma would complain when we were in the house doing nothing and she'd complain when we'd leave the house. I sighed; laying there I couldn't help but think about where my life was going. I didn't want to live the life my mother lived; seeing how she was now scared me. I didn't want to cling onto the wounds of the past and didn't want my happiness to be crippled by them.

Yuma was allowing our extended family to control her happiness and her decisions. That wasn't the life I wanted to live.

Getting up, I continued my morning routine before walking into my mother's room and catching her at her habitual scene: Drinking coffee while peacefully looking out the window. The air was heavy with the scent of her drink, making me feel that I was walking into a Starbucks.

"*Sabah al khair* (good morning) Yuma" I said before inviting myself into her bed, she looked at me without any expression, sipped her coffee and responded, "*Sabah el noor.*" I just stared at her for a minute or two, taking in my mother's features.

Yuma is a very beautiful woman for her age. Even though, at the time, she was in her 40's, she didn't look a day past 30. Many say I look identical to her except that I have bigger eyes and a curvier body. I felt honored to look like her--to look like a woman who had survived so much trauma in her life and who still found a reason to wake up every-day, even if it was just to pay bills. She was my rising sun greeting me in the morning; the proud moon as it glows amongst the darkness sur-rounding it; the smell of freshly mowed grass; the tune of spring as it approaches; and the dance of the rain as it arrives swiftly and silently gracing the earth with its presence. She is everything amazing and yet subtle that is in this life. To me, she is everything--God's greatest gift to mankind, which is why heaven lay beneath her feet and that I felt she held life's ultimate purpose.

"Yuma?" I asked after realizing I was staring at her for far too long. The wind blew in slightly causing the curtains to part and brush our arms softly, letting us know the universe was also a part of this conversation.

"Huh?" she asked before taking another sip.

"What was it like growing up for you? In a home of fourteen?" I remembered when Yuma first told me she had nine sisters and two brothers. I couldn't wrap my head around the fact that my 4'11" grand-mother had birthed that many kids! Those must have been some huge family Ramadan dinners they prepared.

"We were poor; I was always working to help support our family. I would go to school, work and then home and not spend any time with my friends."

"But you had fun, though right?"

Yuma looked pained then, "Amani I don't want to talk about it, the past makes me sad."

"Why?"

"Because I miss my family."

"Then why don't you just speak to them?"

"Things are different now, you don't understand. As you age, the things that are important to you will change; your parents and siblings will be second to your nuclear family, slowly becoming detached and forgetting me is normal."

I shook my head then, "That can't be true, I don't find myself ever forgetting about you Yuma."

She shook her head then, "Amani, you're in college and you don't call me or see me in weeks because you're focused on your future. What happens when you get married and start a family?"

I said nothing then; the mere thought of a life without my mother was unbearable. It pained me to think she wouldn't be a daily sight for sore eyes. But she was right. In college, I already lived day to day without seeing or speaking to her.

I remained silent then, listening as cars drove by and children giggled and chased one another down the sidewalk. This moment was nothing special to speak of and yet it was this very moment, strung along with other simple, uneventful days that made a chain of memories I'd fondly look over in the future like a jeweler inspecting his inventory. These memories would become a piece that, like an antique, carried a stained and aged imprint that will carry on for a lifetime to come.

And silence...it was scary in the sense that we keep ourselves busy, so that it would never be able to catch up to us and yet, it finds us still. It bombards you without warning at times, giving you no choice but to face it. Your thoughts encompass you, the world drains away and there is no visual distraction, only reflection. Many of us are not ready to face our own thoughts that we allow to float in our minds freely, thus when they arrive, a feeling of dread overcomes us.

Aside from the tedious everyday thoughts concerning what is next on your to-do list, there are those thoughts that we may not have the answers to, which make up the black hole we cower from. The unknown, the unplanned...we try our best to make sure that we know what is ahead of us without realizing that what may be ahead may only be an illusion of what we'll face.

Silence scared me because the thoughts I didn't want to think about overwhelmed me. Zoning out, I'd swim in the depths of my thoughts, emerging drenched with whispers of my memories and future endeavors. I wanted nothing more than to run from it all, but there was so much more the future had in store for me that I wasn't yet aware of.

So, for the time being I held on--held onto the silence of today, hoping it would lead me through tomorrow.

CHAPTER 15

History

"A people without the knowledge of their past history,
origin and culture is like a tree without roots."

– Marcus Garvey

H istory is a funny thing, the way it attaches to you and over time becomes a part of you. Our live moments collect themselves as memories, get processed, stored and then filtered through our brains so that we may keep the thoughts worth remembering and dispose of those that aren't. We carefully stash our memories away until we find the need to bring them out, dust them off and review them whenever we feel nostalgic. Sometimes it seems that we are a living and breathing collection of scrapbooks of moments that occupy our brain until we are but a name and a date on a tombstone. Many feel pressured to pass on a legacy so that they are remembered and looked up to by those they leave behind--so that their "scrapbooks" become useful or important enough to keep around and flip through.

I also find the idea of sharing ones' scrapbook with another, inter-esting. In a book, for instance, we can simply write our memories out and relive them word by word, moment by moment and describe it so well, with so much emotion, that the onlooker feels as though they were there. Goosebumps may actually form across the canvas of their skin as the memory washes over them and then, suddenly, they can see the memory as if they were there. As humans, we are lucky to be able to share our books with others, for no other creature alive has the ability to do so. Isn't that magnificent? To allow others to delve into your world, the watercolor of emotions spilling across their scrapbooks leaving evidence of the journey you allowed them to go on with you. That journey stays with you, giving you a different perspective on life than you had before.

But within the scrapbook of my mind, there were a few pages that remained blank--the fabric of its pages devoid of memories or emotions. I contemplated for so long what those missing pieces were, why they were blotted out and where to start my search for them. It wasn't until I sat down with Yuma one evening that I realized she was the key to my missing information. There was so much about her that I did not know; her scrapbook was something she hid from us--not even a glance did we get of it. I was always curious to know more about her, to know what lay within her pages that made her who she was today. But whenever it came time to share, it was as if she checked out, receding into the confines of her room and leaving a distance between us that grew with each passing day.

It bothered me that she was my parent and yet, I knew nothing about her childhood or adolescent life. I often wondered if many of the habits I couldn't shake were habits she also couldn't shake growing up. I would observe other Arab girls and watch their body language around their parents, noticing that many of them often displayed the same barrier my siblings and I did with those who had birthed and raised us. It left a void within us--a broken wire. How could I love someone I didn't know? All I knew was what I saw; all I knew was that she had raised me, fed me, and groomed me to aim for higher education. But she rarely ever opened up. The need to know more about her consumed me as I wondered about the origins of her "scrapbook. I wondered about the significant experiences of her life and their impact as she lived, day by day.

I knew other families in America enjoyed sharing their history with their children. The way the children listened in awe and wonder as stories of events unfolded before them, understanding what the past was like. I could sense a level of intimacy between the parent and child, whereas, I was only told to love a man I visited in prison most of my life. How does a child learn to do that?

I recall staring at Alzalim across the table, knowing this was the man that I called father, but I didn't feel an emotional connection. This fact made me more uncomfortable as the years went on and I grew to become more aware of what was happening around me. He knew nothing about me beside the fact that I enjoyed writing and that my skill set with words was an accomplishment on its own.

Year after year, *polaroids* stacked up with dates and months scribbled across the border with a corny message at the bottom, reminding us that he was thinking of us. But was it wrong that I didn't think of him? That I didn't give the respect he was supposed to have from his children? I felt no obligation to him, no duty to serve or protect him. He was an unknown contributor to my birth--it's all I knew and cared to know as I grew older. I never cared to acquire any knowledge of his history; he didn't seem important enough for me to waste any energy on. The sooner I forgot about his existence, the better, and it was becoming easier and easier to forget him as the days rolled by.

But who was Yuma? How is it that I love this woman so much and what she represents, yet I know nothing of her? This woman whom I've become so strongly attached to is a person I'd fight to the ends of the Earth for. She is a woman I aspire to be like--a role model and mother I wish to one day be like. How is it I was so obsessed with someone whose past was nothing but a mystery? What mistakes had she made in her lifetime that made her who she was today? Which scrapbook memories had meant the most to her and which ones were too painful to speak about in the moment? I wanted to know more about the mother who had carried me for seven months and brought me into this world. As I grew more anxious to know such details and as I stared at her, she remained the puzzle that always was. I'd ask her many questions hoping she'd open up bit by bit with me, but she wouldn't budge, repeatedly insisting that the past was the past and there was nothing left to it.

I felt incomplete being oblivious of my mother's history. What were the pieces of me that were a part of her? It's as if our histories sit side by side on a bookshelf, but I would never be able to analyze her pages and understand the woman that had influenced my perspective on life--because her pages were kept hidden. Torn out, faded away, unspoken, and disposed of, her scrapbook would remain next to mine on a shelf, collecting dust as I held onto our relationship with nothing but blind faith.

PART TWO

CHAPTER 16

The Calm Before the Storm

"It is better to meet danger than to wait for it. He that
is on a lee shore, and foresees a hurricane, stands out to
sea and encounters a storm to avoid a shipwreck."

– Charles Caleb Colton

When you're young and you come across conflict of any sort, you know something's wrong--but you may not know what. Confused, you may either hide in fear or approach the problem. You can decide to either let it pass or come face to face with conflict, in hopes that maybe it'll stop. We don't realize the courage we have as kids in such instances or the impact that these encounters have on us in the process of our development. We are young warriors deciding whether we'll stand and fight or run and hide away before our conscious minds are able to understand it. At such a time in our development, fear can either break your identity or solidify it.

Growing up, my siblings and I were faced time and time again with violence and fear, choosing which battles to sit out and hide from, and the ones to stand our ground in. To us, it all depended on what we were fighting for and as we got older; we all were fighting for one thing, and that thing, in turn, was a person: Our mother.

The release of my father from prison was, for us, similar to a jump off a cliff, where a person knows that rock bottom was going to inevitably come but they were never sure when. It was anxiety- filled, knowing that what the moments we endured weren't, in fact, the worst they could be, and that thought alone scared us more than the violence we were put through.

There were times when one of many of my father's side girlfriends would call our home and ask for him. I was always unsure of whether or not they knew he was married with four kids, but at that age, I was too afraid to confront him about it. My older sister, on the other hand (who I looked up to most of my childhood), was fearless during the reign of our father in the household. The courage she carried also carried our family; she was who we turned to whenever we were afraid, including my mother. As much as Yuma would not like to admit it, she fed off Ilham's courage and tried to use it as best she could.

One day Ilham wasn't having it with these women calling our house, so she took the phone from my Yuma's hands. "Hi, do you know this is his daughter speaking to you on the phone?" She asked angrily into the phone.We were in the kitchen then--it was the middle of summer and the heat slowly wavered in the air, joining us in the turmoil that was about to ensue. The sun shone brightly outside, peeking through the windows of the house that would allow it access to our dim lives. The smell of freshly mowed grass filled the air, along with the sound of children laughing as they played hopscotch or swung hula-hoops around themselves. My mother tried grabbing the phone from my sister, fear and sadness filling her eyes. I knew she was afraid of what would happen once my father found out--she was always afraid. I didn't blame her, but my sister didn't care; she didn't like seeing the people she loved hurt or distressed.

"Yes, and the woman who was on the phone with you earlier was his WIFE; oh and he has three other kids! One happens to be 4 years old! Mhmm...hmm...so stop calling..." *Beep.*

I stood there as my heart raced, knowing no good could come of this, but so proud of her for doing it at the same time. We all sensed a deep sadness in Yuma; we saw how hurt she was having to deal with the constant cycle of women coming in and out of our lives, making her feel that she was never good enough. We saw how she looked at herself in the mirror and the constant scrutiny she put herself through. We felt sadness growing heavy within us, knowing that, being hurt by someone you love, by someone you gave everything to, and abandoned your family abroad for--that kind of love was deeply rooted within the core of one's heart. Love gone unrequited and betrayed by the man or whomever you've given your heart to--that wound takes a toll and changes you even if you didn't wish it.

There was nothing we could do about what my sister did. We had no choice but to wait for what was to come next. There were many times I felt that our lives would be too much for even a reality TV show, because the things that happened to us were too real. We weren't paid to make drama happen; it just happened whether we wanted it to or not. And I hated it, to always feel my heart racing and skipping a beat with ample amounts of adrenaline pumping through my bloodstream. In my family, my sister and I were always on our toes because there was always something happening that would try to destroy us. To live with that fear continually wasn't healthy and we all knew it. So, we did what we did best--we waited.

· · · · ·

A few hours had gone by then and still there was no sign of Alzalim. I felt relieved thinking that maybe he went on one of his long trips again and wouldn't return for a few months...or the rest of his life. But I spoke too soon.

The door slammed open with the force of an angry giant, "*Alya!!!!!!!*" Alzalim yelled. Yuma sat upstairs quietly in her bed. His eyes were bulging out of his head and he wore that crazed look on his face that only the devil could supply a man with. The veins in his eyes were bloodshot as he scanned the room.

Ilham, Ayman, and I were sitting in the living room doing absolutely nothing while Nur was upstairs in the comfort of Yuma's arms. My heart began pounding so incredibly hard that I was sure everyone could hear the frenetic organ sounding off an alarm to run, though not a single soul paid any mind to it, not even its owner. The three of us sat there in fear, none of us making eye contact with him, knowing it would only set him off further.

"*ALYA!!*" He roared ever so loudly,

"What?!" Yuma yelled back, feigning confidence. The front door slammed shut, shaking the house with the reverberations encompassing the walls and floors. I was trembling in fear knowing the harm and danger our father could bring. I just didn't know what to do next...I was afraid.

He stood there for what seemed like an eternity before he climbed up the stairs. My heart leapt, screaming at me to protect our mother. My sister and I both shot up the stairs after him. My body was fully awakened and ready for battle, our mission was always the same. Never let him hurt her, never.

I was beyond terrified and so afraid that my body shook and my vision blurred. I knew what fear felt like for me; I knew what it did to my body and the after effects my body went through when fear was in my system for too long. This wasn't a good idea going in, but then again, the pairing of my parents wasn't good to begin with either.

Ilham and I arrived just in time; she took the lead and placed herself at the door ready to leap in if the need arose. I nervously stood beside her and watched as the events that happened next unfolded.

"Why'd you call Brittany? Why do you butt your nose in my business?!!" He yelled furiously.

Ilham grabbed Nur and told her to head downstairs before any harm could come to her. Although confused, Nur obliged given that Ilham was like a mother to her. She scurried past me and shuffled her way down the stairs, as Yuma slowly crawled out of bed and met his stare.

"What's none of my business? The fact that my husband is parading himself with these hookers and bitches?! Or the fact that they're calling MY house that I pay the bills for?! Or the fact that you have NO shame showing your children how low of a man you are?!! Have some dignity for the name you carry for this family!"

"If you don't shut your mouth..." he began yelling as he scowled and raised his hand to slap her.

Ilham jumped in between them then."Don't you touch her!" she yelled.

I took in that sight, wishing only that I could replicate the image from my memories to show the world how magnificent and brave she looked--words don't do her justice. She stared fear in the face so viciously, and with so much fire, that her bravery was contagious.

I went to my mother's side pushing her behind me and further away from him. Standing behind Ilham, I also grimaced at Alzalim, who then shifted his deadly gaze onto my sister and I.

"Get out."

"No," we both replied simultaneously.

"Get out!"

"No!" We yelled.

"Ilham, Amani, go; this isn't your business," our mother's voice ordered. She was calm, but you could feel how afraid she was. There was no way we'd let him touch her, not one bit.

"Listen to your mother and get out," he ordered.

"No. What? You're mad that we caught you? Or that you lost your girlfriend? You should be ashamed of who you are. Bringing someone like that around Nur," Ilham retorted. The cheerleader in my mind was so happy to see Ilham give him the side of the story he was lacking from his family. I almost laughed.

"Ilham watch your mouth, he's still your father!" Yuma yelled.

Ilham laughed then, "No, he's not, my father is dead to me".

Tensions were heavy, our father knew that Ilham wouldn't back down from being our savior. She was noble and headstrong, having inherited her stubbornness from him. His eyes grew massive, the insanity in them unchecked, as the anger coursed through them with fury. It felt as though time stood still during the events that happened next, over which I could not believe my eyes.

Hand raised, he grabbed a fist full of Ilham's hair and snapped her neck at an angle. Memories of her as a kid being tortured by Yuma flashed in my mind. I was beginning to panic, unsure of what to do.

"Let her go!!" I screamed making a move to lunge at him, Yuma restrained me with an iron grip,

"This is between them, it is her battle to overcome."

"Yuma he's hurting her though!"

"Get the hell off me!" Ilham ordered with malice; grabbing his arm, she began fighting back, punching him square in the face. No one in my family has ever dared go against my father due to his history and size, so I considered Ilham a true badass for challenging him the way she did.

Nur began crying hysterically, her wails reaching pitches higher than I believed she could manage. Her face exploded with red color, eyes soaked, and lashes heavy with tears. She reached out to Ilham who was now in a full fist fight with Yaba.

Ilham was holding up against Alzalim for awhile, but his frame overpowered her. Putting her in a neck lock triggered her screams for Yuma to help her. Her face was bruising now, lip bleeding, and hair disheveled. Ilham looked like one of those abused puppies that made you cry on the spot. I hated seeing her like this; whenever she was sad, she always had this face that really made you want to give her the world to see her happy again. And this time, he was causing her that pain.

"Yuma help me! I can't breathe!" she begged; I looked behind me willing Yuma to stop the madness. Instead, she took a step back and shook her head,

"No, you disrespected your father. I'm ashamed to help you."

"What!" I screamed not comprehending the crap that came from her mouth. I was in complete panic, with an adrenaline rush confused as to where it should go. The alarms in my body where going off every-where: My brain, my heart, my lungs. I couldn't think, all I know is that Ilham needed help. *Screw my fear,* I decided. Turning around, I ran into the next room to help her and was interrupted by her body erupting in a spasm. At this point, Yaba released his grip on her, causing her body to fall limp to the ground with the spasms continuing. He sat there for a moment watching the work he'd created before walking out of the room, content with his abuse.

Collapsing beside her, I held her head in my lap, and my hair fell past my face to her cheek. My face was also submerged in oceans of tears. Ilham's eyes registered fear--immense fear. Cradling her, as I choked on my worry, I cried and screamed for Yuma to help. I was terrified Ilham was dying. Yuma never came.

"YUMA SHE COULD BE DYING! SHE DID THIS TO PROTECT YOU!"

Rocking Ilham, I hugged her tightly as her spasms became less and less frequent. Her breathing was now labored and her face was drenched in tears--both hers and mine. I hugged her head tightly and apologized over and over for not knowing what to do. She remained silent, with her labored breathing being the only thing breaking the silence. Raising her hand to me, she indicated that both her ring and pinky finger were broken. The bastard had injured her.

"Amani go," he ordered, trying to appeal to the weakest of the group. I shook my head no, to which he gave a hard look.

"Don't talk to them," Yuma yelled. "It's your fault, this is all your fault."

He began to pace then, back and forth, back and forth. I was nervous, sweat starting to appear and my hands getting slick. I was exhausted--totally mentally exhausted from all this.

"You know what?" He said, breaking the silence. He went over to my mom's dressers, grabbing her clothes and throwing them out the window. One by one, piles of her clothes were being thrown out.

"Alzalim!!" Yuma yelled, "Stop!! Those are my clothes."

"All of you get out of my house; get your clothes and get out!"

"Are you crazy?! Kick me out that's fine, but these are your kids!"

"They're not my kids, they're a bunch of bitches," he responded venomously with spit spraying those in his vicinity.

So much started happening before we had time to process the events that were unfolding. In a matter of minutes, all of Yuma's clothes were spread out outside with Ilham's stuff following suit, and mine to soon follow after. He was going on a rampage and continued to swear under his breath, as our neighbors peered at the commotion he was creating. Immediately, Yuma headed downstairs with Nur rushing to pick up her clothes from the sidewalks and the street. I could feel the thud of my heart beating carelessly against my chest, pressing itself against the walls of my inside, as if to plead with me to run.

But, I could not.

Amongst the fear and sadness, there was a glimmer of courage and it begged me to stay alongside my sister and fight. We were angry, extremely angry and we wanted nothing more than to rid our lives of the man we had to call father.

Looking down, I saw the soldier who proudly stood up for her family: Ilham. She went head to head with him and stood firmly in her place, with eyes full of hate. He towered over her with a look just as menacing, and it was then that I truly saw what everyone saw in my sister. I saw why they said she reminded them of my father; she was fearless, even in the face of danger. She was as mortal as any human could be, yet, she was a warrior standing to fight this battle rather than turn away with her tail tucked between her legs. She was truly a sight to see--magnificent and strong.

The air felt prickly, as if we were in a sea of needles and pins. The hair on the back of my neck stood on its ends, because what was yet to come was unknown.

Angry, Yuma stormed back into the house and onto the porch, yelling at our father, saying that he did not have the power to remove us from the household. Calling our grandmother, she caught her up about the situation that occurred within our home. The streets surrounding us were swarming with activity, onlookers watching us outside their windows as children watched on the corner of the streets, and sat balanced on their bikes and strollers.

Usually, the neighborhood was alive with action; if you sat outside long enough, you'd be able to see evictions, divorces, prostitute exchanges, drug deals happening, and the occasional crackhead roaming around. I wouldn't say our neighborhood was dangerous; it was more so alive and pulsating with poverty and free entertainment if you couldn't afford cable. Usually our family kept our heads indoors and kept our business amongst ourselves, but on this day, our father practically invited the neighborhood to watch the drama unfold.

Just then our aunt pulled up in her vehicle with the head of the community, or as I call it: "the mafia." Siti (grandmother) had a presence around her--this aura that screamed in your face--which was felt before she even approached the scene. Her embodiment screamed out 'boss' or 'important'. Whatever she said went; there were no ifs, ands, or buts about it. Growing up, I never felt that looming fog she carried because I was still naive; I still believed she cared for our family and did her best to look out for us. But in time, I became more aware of why she truly needed us: We were her trophy family. She would parade us in the faces of others if the occasion called for it, because my older sister and I were college students with bright futures ahead of us. She'd raised a family of failures and this was her way to redeem herself. Of course, she would never admit to that, because she wanted us under her thumb at all times; whenever anyone so much as sneezed the wrong way she ruined their reputation before the sneeze arrived.

The car door opened and emerging from its air-conditioned atmosphere stood an elderly woman standing at 5 feet tall. She was probably in her late 60's. I was unsure of her age and truth be told, still am. But she carried no limp in her walk, no cane, and needed no help whatsoever. She was the most fit grandmother I knew and she did everything all on her own without the assistance of the government or her family. She was a boss, which is why she called the shots. Her face was always the same, straight lipped, high cheekbones that made her beauty ageless; her straight posture was so intact, that when I was younger, I swear I thought she belonged to a royal family. Her beauty was clear and so subtle that hearing she had once been a model in her 20's, I didn't doubt it. Even at this age she was still a beautiful woman. She wore a traditional, middle eastern decorated dress: Black with red, gold and green embroidery of small flowers and leaves. She wore the same hijab (headscarf) that she always wore which was just simply a black headscarf. She headed straight to my sister who she was furious with. Yuma walked up to her and greeted her with two kisses, one on each cheek.

Within our culture, it was customary and a sign of respect to greet others by saying, "*Salam wa alaikum*," (greetings, may peace be upon you). Women greeted each other with two kisses, one on each cheek. If the woman who you are greeting is older than you and dear to you, you would kiss them on each cheek and then take their right hand, kiss the top of their hand, and then bring it to your forehead until it touches it gently. You would do that three times, respectively. If a woman was greeting a man, they would simply say, "*ASA*," and then shake hands as to respect the gender differences and avoid any other contact with their bodies. Men greeting men would greet one another with, "*ASA*," and then, either a kiss on the cheek or a simple handshake.

Ilham managed to find the strength to get up and greet Siti, as I did, alongside her. As my sister and mother were informing her of the events that previously took place, Alzalim watched from inside with a look in his eye, that sort of sparkled in a way that told me he enjoyed seeing the rage he caused, watching the family breakdown in different ways. Yuma was furious, Ilham was injured, Nur was crying, Ayman was locked in his room not partaking in any of this, and I was watching everything unfold, admittedly scared. It angered me that he'd caused so much frustration and drama all because he lost another 'hoe'. I always think that there is no possible room for me to hate him further than I already did, but somehow, he always managed to raise the bar. I hated myself more for being afraid of him.

Siti then walked into the house, taking in the mess that he caused. She glared at him then, "What in the name of hell are you doing?! Do you see this scene you're causing?!"

"Ilham answered my phone call, yelling to Brit that I had a wife and kids!!" he retorted.

"And?! You do; stop acting like a child and let them back in before someone calls the cops. It's enough you dragged me out here for something this ridiculous, but now the whole neighborhood is watching and your baby girl! Get yourself together and help them bring everything back in! Putting your hands on your eldest is shameful! You are supposed to protect her! Not endanger her!!" She scolded him. The anger in her face showed and he did well not to respond.

Siti started mumbling under her breath as she took the scene in again and went to my sister, "And you," she pointed to her, "don't get involved with your father's business; you're a lady so you need to act like one. We don't go yelling at our fathers in the streets like some kind of animal; carry yourself with some respect! See to it that this gets treated, the audacity of the man to lay his hands on his full grown daughter."

Ilham was angry but she couldn't help but laugh as she said, "I don't care Siti, he needs to stop acting like a teenage kid and go do whatever the hell he wants; what about Nur?!"

The wind picked up then--a sign that a storm was coming. Siti sighed and walked closer to Ilham with a smile, "What are you going to do? He's like this, you just have to accept it, it's what men do".

I remember rolling my eyes then. Accept it....why were his actions always justified for this reason? Why did we just simply have to accept it? We were a sinking ship and her words only sealed our fate. We would go under the waves and no one would hold him responsible for the lives lost at sea. Wasn't the captain supposed to go down with his ship?

CHAPTER 17

Useless

"Life is 10% what happens to you and 90% how you react to it."

– Charles R. Swindoll

Have you ever made a promise to someone with the full intent to make good on that promise? Did you believe that there was no way you could break it? But then the unexpected happens and the promise has been broken with a symbolic pact of your words shattering and dissipating into nothingness. You then feel like a fraud and that everything you worked for to make sure your word was dependable has now been undone. You are no longer reliable, no longer needed, and you become useless.

On an early fall day, I realized just how useless my word had become when the one I loved the most was in danger. I was no hero and no protector; I was, simply put, an engine without fuel and was running out of gas. To avoid any confusion, let me start from the beginning.

It was a few weeks into the new fall semester of 2015. Finally, I was able to leave my home and get away from the drama there. I had already moved into my first off campus apartment with four other roommates, who happened to be my sorority sisters. It was nice to live in a house and not a dorm room that had alarms going off in the dead of night all the time. The early morning sun was eagerly shining inside each and every household, on this particular Saturday morning I decided it would be a day to lounge around in bed all day and do nothing. I was drained from all the readings I had to get done for my psychology courses that suffocated me daily. I needed to relax--it was a priority of mine.

My room was so bright, open, and airy that it made me feel alive. Normally I hated the bright pink paint and a fake brick wall separating my roommates' room from mine. But the sun peeking through the curtains of my room made it look simply beautiful. I decided to lay back in bed and enjoy this rare moment I had to myself. I closed my eyes and began to fall back into a slumber. However, a vibration brought me back from the land of slumber and dreams, along with the iconic iPhone ringtone that belonged to my cell phone. Slowly I peeled my eyelids open and shifted my head to my left where my iPhone lay on the nightstand. I slowly reached for my phone, still a bit sluggish from sleep, and answered without looking at the caller ID.

"Hello?"

"Hello," my dad's voice echoed back; I shot up quicker than expected then. As if conditioned, my heart rate increased. I jumped out of bed and looked out the two windows from my bedroom. There seemed to be no sign of him which was good. I hadn't informed him that I was living off campus, or in an apartment, with four other women. I didn't want to risk him asking for my address because I simply didn't want any surprise visits from him.

"Yea?" I asked, nonchalantly.

"Do you want to visit Hasib with Ilham today?" He asked, as children were calling his attention in the background. It was most likely my cousins that came from overseas that wanted to be driven around by him.

"Yea, I guess why not. I haven't seen him in forever". Hasib was my dad's oldest brother, and my favorite uncle. As a child, I secretly looked up to him as a father because my biological one was nowhere in sight. In addition, he carried more light than my father ever did. He had a heart of pure gold and he really made you smile, genuinely smile, because that's all he wanted from you. Not your money or your pain--he simply just wanted to see you smile and what could be more honorable than that?

He was the only Abdel Nour I actually loved. I truly and deeply loved him more than any other and looked up to him. He was what I wanted my husband to be like. With a gentle heart and kind words, his humanity embodied what it meant to be a man. He was truly the definition of a hero in my book. His immediate family owned a couple of corner stores and houses that they rented out and he'd always give the poor food from his inventory, regardless of the fact that it would hurt his business in the long run. He believed that whatever you put into the universe, you'd receive back, later in the future. These were thoughts and actions I would soon began to live by, as well.

"Meet up with Ilham and we'll pick you up," he requested, seeming uninterested. I rolled my eyes as I tried to calm my racing heart with the sound of his voice sending chills throughout my body.

"Okay," I responded, waiting a second or two before hanging up the phone. The silence felt nice, with the warm sun and the calming sounds of summer ending, I felt content.

Although the sound of my dad's voice upset me, it didn't ruin the fact that I would get to see my favorite uncle. It had been a long while since I last saw my uncle and being that he was now in a halfway house where inmates who were eligible for release with parole were kept for a short period, he was closer to being home than he was a year ago. I was thrilled and contacted Ilham to make sure I knew where to meet her.

We decided to meet at the nearest Dunkin Donuts in which we caught up and both commented on the dread we felt talking to our father. We had some time to kill, so we ordered some coffee and donuts to dine on, as we discussed our future plans and career options.

Ten minutes after our arrival, Ilham received a call from Najwa (my uncle's wife) and I grimaced at the sight of her name appearing on Ilham's phone screen. Najwa was probably the worst woman alive, by far the evilest, and in desperate need of a wardrobe change. Her heart was filled with coal and regrets. She was constantly on the lookout of my family, always wanting to ruin our family name or reputation, so that the community would frown upon us. I never understood why she hated our family so much. Did she hate my mother because Yuma was more attractive or a better wife than she was? Or did she hate our mother because her husband was so friendly with Yuma? Or that Yuma raised successful kids and of none of Najwa's nine kids that she bore went to college? Whatever it was, with age, I began to despise the woman because she didn't seem to mind her business, she didn't have much of a life or even dreams to begin with. Yea, you own a couple of houses and have a bunch of corner stores that you aren't happy with and you don't carry the joy your husband does. It was all simple really, she did whatever she needed to bring in money, and with seven boys and two girls consistently eating, I don't blame her.

She pulled up in her black SUV with music blaring out the windows for the early Marshal street wanderers to enjoy. Getting up, with no rush at all, we headed outside and into her vehicle which was parked outside the coffee shop. After greeting her, we sat silently while Najwa screamed on the phone about a repair to one of her houses that was incorrectly done during the entire car ride to our house. We were allowed to pick

Nur up so that she was able to see her uncle, as well. In total, there was five of us in the car going to see Hasib: Najwa, her daughter, Ilham, Nur and myself.

I was filled with excitement in anticipation of seeing my uncle Hasib, I had not seen him in what seemed like forever and I went over all the details I wanted to catch him up on. Ilham and I had grown so much since we'd last seen him and he always showed genuine excitement in seeing us the way a father would.

Najwa looked in the mirror in which she could clearly see us over-joyed in the background and asked without the slightest smile, "You guys excited to see your uncle?"

"Yea," Ilham and I responded with the same enthusiasm she showed us. I did my best to ignore her attitude and the dislike she carried for us that she didn't care to hide. She rubbed me entirely the wrong way and every second I was near her, it only made me angrier.

Soon enough, we pulled into the parking lot where Nur jumped out of the vehicle and started singing, "*We're going to see Hasib, we're going to see Hasib.*" Ilham and I smiled at the enjoyment she showed to see her uncle.

Najwa's daughter Jamila stepped out of the vehicle, as well, and I got a good look at her then. I had not seen her in about a year or two and the change in her appearance hit me in the face. Sadly, she looked like one of her brothers; her face was chubby, and her cheeks were red--not rosy, but so red it looked like a rash. She was obese now, no sign of the girly girl we all admired and adored when she was younger. She wore clothes big enough to drown in and her hair was tied back in a very unflattering way.

I pitied her then; like her brothers, she had to remain in the corner stores or roam around with her mother all day, so she was always sur-rounded by junk food. Her mother never cooked and I'm pretty sure it's because she didn't know how to. My cousin's fate wasn't her own and for that my heart went out to her. She didn't have a proper role model, she wouldn't be able to understand what a healthy lifestyle was or learn to love herself the way she should, because her mother restricted her from so much. She looked angry as she walked past Ilham and I, not bothering with a hello or a how are you; I was shocked to see how she adopted her mother's personality and the hate she held for us. I was beginning to sense that she was no longer the sweet girl we all knew and loved and was now beginning to become tainted by her mother's hatred to the world around her. It was a path I didn't want for her-- a path I knew she didn't know, at the moment, would become her downfall if she continued to pursue it.

Entering the small halfway house, we signed in and removed any and all metal or jewelry. My heart thudded in my chest knowing that my uncle was right past those doors. It was an exhilarating feeling, given that he was the only Abdel Nour family member I was proud to admit I missed and adored. Walking through the metal sensors, I felt happy for the first time in a while. Hasib was the only family member I didn't feel stressed when visiting. Everything was just so effortless with him; he was light hearted, airy and fun. He didn't like drama, nor did he condone it. I could swear he was the manifestation of light itself; he was an angel and I loved him so much. I really did.

Walking in, I heard him shout in excitement, "Hey, my girls are here!" Then I heard his laugh. His laugh had made me jump in excitement as a child, because when I was younger and lived with Siti, it was one of the first things I heard before I ran out and into his arms to which he'd say, "How are you *habibti* (sweetie)?"

"I'm doing well," I said now smiling. He squeezed me so tight in his bear hug that I had to stop myself from crying so quickly. He was a breath of fresh air that I needed desperately.

He stepped back and looked at us with a wide smile and adoring eyes, "Mash'Allah (God has willed--a term used to appreciate the work of God), you girls are BEAUTIFUL! You've grown up so much and Nur! You're so beautiful habibti!" he remarked, as he picked her up and planted kisses all over her cheeks. "Those eyes of yours Mash'Allah are gorgeous!!" Hasib exclaimed about Nur. Ilham and I smiled then; our family was indeed blessed with good looks, not realizing it until we saw his own family. He's always told us that he viewed us as his children just as much as his own. I always believed that he secretly wanted my siblings and I as his own; there was a love in his eyes that he had for us when he saw us--a look I never saw when he looked at his own children.

I noticed he didn't kiss his wife or even pay her any mind for that matter. Their marriage seemed to be on the rocks and I could sense no emotion between them. What shocked me further was how he kissed his daughter, hugged her, and then proceeded to pay attention to my sisters and I. I was curious to know what happened there and I could see she was beginning to get jealous that Nur was receiving all the attention from her father.

"How's school? What have you guys been up to? It's been such a long time; I want to know everything!" He remarked, eagerly and with such a glow, that the entire room lit up. Ilham began telling him about the life of an international relations major and the plans she set for herself for the near future, as she saw it. He clung onto every word she said and was so proud that he couldn't stop smiling.

"So, are you going straight to law school when you graduate?" he asked.

"That's the plan; I'm doing a lot of research about where I want to go right now, but I'm looking into D.C.," she confirmed.

"That's amazing! So grown up now;, where has time gone?! Your father must be so proud."

Ilham and I rolled our eyes to which he dropped his smile and sighed, "Girls, listen: I know your father isn't right in the head, but he loves you, he really does. I remember speaking to him and the regret he feels about not being in your lives is there; I felt how sad he was, and he told me you guys would never forgive him"

"And he's right," Ilham and I exclaimed simultaneously. We glanced at one another before laughing and then composed ourselves when we saw how disappointed he looked.

I sighed then, "Look, you can't say we didn't try. We aren't kids anymore; we don't need his love, his satisfaction, his attention for that matter. We don't care, and you can't blame us for that. All these excuses you guys are making for him are just piling on. Goodness, he's a grown man now and he's still too proud to own up to his mistakes to our faces. He doesn't regret anything; if he truly meant it, he would have worked hard to change".

My uncle turned to me then and took my hand, "Habibti, listen to me: People make mistakes and some more than others. That doesn't mean you can't learn to forgive them. Look at me, I've been here for 10 years and my kids forgave me."

"That's because you're an innocent man," I retorted. "Innocence is forgiven; the acts of the devil aren't."

He looked at us with such sadness, knowing that no matter what he said, nothing would change. We hated our father; you could feel it whenever his name was mentioned.

"How are you Amani?" He asked wanting to hear what I'd been up to as of late.

"Well, I switched my major to human science and family development. I think I may want to be a counselor, but I'm not sure yet. I started a novel though; it's about the life Yuma lived through my eyes. I'm telling the story of struggle she's had being in a community which twisted

123

our beautiful culture for their own selfish gain and, in turn, hurt Yuma and destroyed her spirit. To be frank, I'm exposing you all."

His eyes grew big and his smile bigger, "That's a great novel to write! I tell you, you have such a way with words, it's scary. You don't need a weapon; your words do it. I remember that email you sent me before, with how disappointed you were with me, and reading it I cried because you didn't need a knife to wound me. I felt everything you wanted me to feel and it hurt!" He exclaimed with such seriousness.

It was true; I wrote him an email a while ago about how disappointed I was with the fact that he allowed his wife to be the way she was without monitoring her or putting her in her place. He was truly afraid of her and I've never seen a man more terrified to disobey his wife. I was fed up with it and let him know just how cowardly his actions were. It hurt him, but I didn't care because he'd allowed such a woman to cause havoc without repercussions.

"Well what can I say, I only said what I felt was true."

He stared at me awhile before laughing, "I love that! You have SUCH a smart mouth! You don't care what you say! You just say it!"

I smiled then, because it was contagious when he was smiling. I was happy, he was happy, and that meant the world to me. I enjoyed seeing his aging eyes smiling along with him. I loved seeing the life flowing through him. It was a wondrous sight to see.

"Mash'Allah you're so beautiful!! I haven't seen you in forever!"

Once more I smiled; he was right. Ilham was more inclined to visit family, given that she loved staying in touch with everyone. I, on the other hand, didn't care to see any Arabs. They rubbed me the wrong way, given that I associated any and all Arabs with my family. Well, at least the ones in Syracuse. I didn't want anyone knowing my life, my plans, or my future. I didn't want any of them to be a part of it. Quite frankly, I was fonder of the carefree American lifestyle, because I wasn't strictly monitored nor did I carry the fate of my family's reputation on my shoulders for that matter. I wanted to fall in love naturally, without arranged engagements, and to be able to go out on my own without anyone thinking I was doing something sinful. I wanted to live on my own without the Arab community thinking I was sinful. I believed Ayman shared my beliefs, as well, given his need to hide away from the world.

"How's Ayman?" He inquired, "I heard he was dating a prostitute."

Ilham became angry then, "Actually, he had no idea she was a prostitute."

"How did he not know? He was dating her; you guys should watch your brother. The things people are saying about him aren't good," his remark followed with a shake of his head in disapproval, lips tucked in, eyes facing down--concern and judgement, written all over his face.

Najwa and Jamila sat silently beside us as Nur played cards with her. I could sense something bad was about to happen, but I didn't know how to end it before it began. I had no idea where it would come from. Or when.

"He didn't know she was one and when he found out, thanks to your son--who by the way used to sleep with her--dumped her, because he deserved better! Funny how your sons are talking shit about our brother when he's never done anything wrong to anybody! He's the one that stays out of all the drama and here you guys go trying to put him in. He's not the one who's been in and out of jail like your sons; he's going to college and he's a smart boy, but of course, you guys want to taint his name too huh?!" Ilham was livid, she was very protective of our family and I was shocked to hear all this, because I had no idea he was dating a prostitute let alone dating. I was so out of touch with my family that I was clueless throughout most of the conversation.

The air became prickly then. It seemed to get ten times hotter and I could hear the thumps of my heart in my ears. A ringing occurred, in and out, that I couldn't distinguish whether it was in my head or in the room. My mouth suddenly became dry and Hasib looked at Ilham with shock.

Just then, Najwa sat up in her chair that she'd silently sat in the entire time, her black aura looming over us now, "Don't talk about my sons like that; this conversation has nothing to do with them, so keep their names out of your mouth!"

"Then keep Ayman's name out of yours; it's *so* funny that you guys can't ever stay out of our business. You always want to make us look bad when we aren't! Just leave us alone."

"I don't care; you keep my children's name the fuck out of your mouth."

My hands became clammy then; I didn't know what to do. Ilham was our protector and she approached this with no fear whatsoever.

"Then keep my brother's name *the fuck* out of your mouths!" She glared at Najwa angrily with hatred that was evident in her eyes. I was afraid, truly afraid, because Najwa was worse than Siti by a thousand times; in fact, she pulled the strings behind Siti's rule over the community. She was the one to truly be afraid of, given that she would demolish someone's reputation and not feel a bit of guilt about it.

Getting up, she started cursing left and right, "So, this is what you let them do huh? This is how you show respect to your wife huh? So help you God, once you get out, keep this up Hasib. I'm going to unleash hell."

She threw a string of insults before taking her daughter and leaving the building. I sat there shocked, given that she was our ride here. If she left we had no way of getting home and what were we to do then? I was annoyed at the fact that she didn't even take Nur with her. Why leave a child behind who had no part in this? How childish are you?

Realizing my stuff was in her car, I shot out of my chair and ran after her. Opening the door, the sun blinded me as I ran to her car; she was about to step in when she saw me and stopped. Approaching the car in a huff, trying to catch my breath, I told her my stuff was in there and that I needed to grab it.

She angrily looked at me before yelling, "You guys are going to get it! You think I don't know things! You think I can't find out about everything you guys do in that University?! I will get my son's girlfriend to find you guys and beat your ass! Just wait! You think I'm fucking done, you got another thing coming, just watch!"

I put my hands up, "I'm just here to get my stuff, that's it. I have no part in this."

"You don't; tell your sister to watch her fucking mouth!" her voice deepened, intending to do well on that promise.

"Okay," I said as I grabbed my belongings and fled like the coward I was. I was disgusted with how afraid I was of her. Disgusted that I LET her get to me this way! I hated it so much!!

The sun beat heavily against my back as I headed back into the building. My body was shaking with nerves and I collapsed in the chair I previously sat in. Ilham was still angry and sat there as if steam and fire were exiting her body. I felt so overwhelmed that I started crying. I asked Ilham why she had to continue, that there was a time and place for battles to be fought and this wasn't the time nor the place to argue the way she had.

She looked at me with disgust, "You're pathetic, you're supposed to stick up for me--for your brother! And yet, you sat there with nothing to say but cry! You have no care for your family. You just care about yourself and making sure she doesn't find stuff out about you!"

I kept my head down; she was right. I was afraid Najwa would look into me--afraid she'd find something so small and stupid that she'd twist it to make it seem like I was losing my integrity as a woman on the campus grounds. I didn't like drama and hated our family drama more than anything, given that they were dangerous people to mess with. It brought me so much stress and anxiety that it crippled me at times. I'd often skip class because I felt like no matter what I did, I was bringing dishonor to them. But like I mentioned before, Ilham was a warrior; she battled when others were too weak to do so. She was a force to be reckoned with and she wouldn't back down if wrong was being done. Our brother was never involved in any drama; he was too exhausted and weak to put the effort or the time into it. The fact that others were spreading crazy rumors about him didn't sit well with us--Ilham just had the courage to fight whereas I had no idea where my backbone was.

"She's *so* mature, how do you leave behind a child who had nothing to do with this? At least bring Nur home. I swear Hasib, I don't know why you're married to her!" Ilham fussed now, nonchalant looking around the empty room. The TV continued playing in the background as Nur sang softly, playing with the toys set up in the corner. The officer watching over the room stood ready, hand on his belt in case things ended up getting worse.

Hasib looked worried and stressed; he tried to calm us down while figuring out how the hell we were going to be brought back home. It seemed that God was looking out for us because the next visitor that walked into the room was someone he knew from his side of the family.

"Oh, thank God, can you please bring my nieces home please? Their ride left them, and I need them safely brought home".

The man who I've never seen before agreed to bring us back; Hasib seemed nervous and kissed us goodbye.

"Make sure you get home safe okay. I'll call you guys later to make sure you got there safely."

"Okay," we both said. Ilham was still heated, while I was trying to compose myself. There were so many emotions running through me that I didn't know which to address first. I was so ashamed and embarrassed with myself that, during the whole car ride home, I could feel Ilham's disappointed gaze on me. I don't blame her--I really don't. I would have been just as ashamed, if not more, had she been so cowardly.

The world was a blur to me as my thoughts consumed me, in spite of the humming of the vehicle traveling on the road, underneath bridges, and past the buzzing of the busy streets. The wind flew in and did its dance inside the car, flinging everyone's hair which would normally catch our attention and smiles. But no such smile was given today-- there were far too many emotions and even more fears on my mind.

Once we got home, Nur jumped out of the car and rushed inside to go and play with her toys. Ilham and I walked in and called for Yuma, but she didn't answer; we tried a few more times and still there was no response.

"Call her cellphone," Ilham ordered. I did as she asked not wanting her to become more upset than she already was. The phone rang continuously before I reached the voicemail inbox. Hanging up, I proceeded to dial her again, and repeatedly. I started to worry then; Yuma always picked up the phone within the first two calls, even if she was at work. She was always on top of her phone calls. Having called her numerous times without an answer was definitely a cause for concern. From Ilham's expression, it was clear she was contemplating what we should do next; pulling her phone out, she dialed our father who also was not answering. Dialing over four times, she still received no response, and that is when we began to truly worry.

Ilham called Siti next, in hopes that she would pick up her phone. "Hello?" she asked, waiting intently for Siti's voice to come on the other line.

"Hello?" our father's voice echoed back. I looked at Ilham then, confused as to why he didn't pick up his phone if he was just going to pick up his mother's phone.

"Alzalim why aren't you answering your cell phone; I've been calling you," Ilham asked.

"I didn't hear it," was his response. I rolled my eyes, *bullshit*.

"Is Yuma there?" Ilham asked. There was a rustling noise, followed by some voices before he answered,

"No, she's not."

"You sure?" Ilham asked, not believing him whatsoever.

"She's not here," he repeated before the click of the phone alerted us that the line had disconnected.

We began to panic. Yuma never went to Siti's house alone anymore--too much drama occurred whenever she went there. We'd all decided that if and when Yuma had to go to Siti's house it was always with either Ilham or myself so we could protect her if need be. We were worried; there was no reason for him to lie to us like that unless something bad was happening and our gut was telling us to run to her house immediately--that our mother was in danger. There was something in his tone that gave away that he knew she was right there with him yet he didn't want us to know, why?

"How are we going to get there?" I asked frantically, "none of us have a car and everyone we know that has a car isn't here." I began to pace back and forth, wondering why on Earth Yuma would go to Siti's house alone! I could literally think of nothing that would bring her to their house.

"A cab," Ilham said, "we can split the cost, but we have to call now because they take forever."

"Okay," I agreed as I nervously called a cab and waited on the line while the ringing went on.

"Taxi On The Go, what can we do for you?" the man on the other end asked.

"Uhhh hi, I need a cab to pick me up at 145 Graves Street."

"145 Graves Street?"

"Yes," I confirmed.

"And uh, where is this going to ma'am?"

"178 Pinenut Street."

"178 Binenut--"

"No, Pinenut with a 'P.'"

"Okay, we'll be there in 30 minutes or less."

"Thank you."

Hanging up the phone, silence seeped through our ears and rang with its singular, white noise. It seemed like an eternity had gone by, as if time stood still, enjoying the torture it brought us. The day was truly beautiful and for it to be ruined by Najwa was something that didn't surprise me, but it definitely wasn't something I was expecting to occur. My body was on edge, half of it shaking while the other half lay limp. I didn't like drama, specifically our family drama that never failed to find us and pull us back in. It was like an annoying ex that felt he still had claim on you no matter how many years had passed. Just when you thought you could live a normal life, just when you thought you could get away from it all and just forget it ever happened, you turn the corner, and there it was waiting for you.

The wiggle of a doorknob caught our attention then--the sound was loud and brought about a feeling so dreadful that filled the atmosphere. I knew before we turned around, before I saw it, it was something dreadful.

The door creaked open slowly and our world came to a halt. We were falling off the edge, falling into the mass expanse of darkness made up of space that is an endless vacuum of secrets and wonders. I wished more than ever to go blind at that moment, because what I was about to see next was something no child should ever have to see--it would stay with me forever. The scene burned its existence in my mind, and on days where I'd zone off in class I'd find myself replaying that moment to remind myself why I hated my family--why I needed to do better for Yuma who deserved better.

My breathing came to a stop as she stumbled in. My heart skipped frantically and out of control as she took a few steps inside the doorway and dropped to the floor. Her clothes were disheveled and torn; her face beaten; eyes swollen with pads of blue and purple, bruised skin around her eyes; blood dripped from her forehead, roaming down the side of her jaw while she lay collapsed and crying on the floor. Whimpers escaped her mouth as she asked God, "Why"--a never ending, one question loop repeated by our mother as she lay at the entrance.

I couldn't breathe; I couldn't move as I took the scene in, I had never seen Yuma like this. She was the rock of the family; she always knew what to do, where to go, when to do things and what to say. She had the ability to predict the future; she always foresaw when things were coming, and knew when to hide and when to fight. How did she allow this to happen to herself; what went wrong? What happened? Tears pooled in my eyes with the sting of disappointment burning my skin. How could we have let this happen to her? Why? Why was our luck like this? Why did something bad always have to happen to our family when we just wanted to be left alone. We stayed out of everyone's business, stayed out of everyone's way, but no matter what we did, we end up eating dirt at the end of it all.

Fraud. You are no longer reliable; no longer needed. You are useless. My thoughts ravished me.

How were we not able to protect the one person in our lives who cared about us? How were we not able to defend the woman who gave us life? This failure was unforgivable; I no longer allowed myself to hold my head up proudly. We failed with the one promise we made to her. My legs felt weak; I hadn't realized I'd collapsed next to her until I was kissing her feet and asking for forgiveness. Ilham was stronger than I. Angry, she demanded to know what happened, and who had dared touch our mother who disturbed no one and nothing. Her voice demanded justice with each word spoken from her mouth.

I didn't want to hear the details; I didn't want to hear who touched her or how defenseless she was against whomever had harmed her. She was a frail woman; aged and depressed she carried no fire within her. She barely had a flame to keep herself going and yet someone was determined to blow it out. Who was that evil?

She lay in my lap as I caressed her head lightly. I was afraid to touch her; I didn't want to bring more harm to her and didn't know which areas on her body were sore. I was in shock to see her like this. I wasn't used to this violence and didn't know how to handle the situation. To see her beautiful face beaten, to see her now like a child needing protection--the way she clung to my body crying, my heart dropped further and further down my stomach.

"Why did you do this to me? Why couldn't you guys keep your mouths shut? No one told you to go with them; no one told you to say anything!" she continued to sob in my lap. I was slowly putting the pieces together before it hit me that this occurred because of the visit we had with Hasib. Najwa was to blame for this.

"What happened?" Ilham and I asked with tears cascading down our faces. We clung onto her, hoping that with some miracle it would heal her.

"I went over to Sitich's (your grandmother's) house because she called me over. When I got there Najwa was there with two of her sons and her daughter. She got in my face and asked me why my daughter was putting her son's name in her mouth," she paused to catch her breath. "I told her my daughters do not speak ill of anyone unless it derives from facts; that if my daughter had spoken ill of her son it was because it was true."

"Aww Yuma," I whimpered, kissing her head softly.

"She slapped me then, and then she started hitting me. I fought back, *wallah*, I fought back," she cried, trying to look up but wincing with pain, "but then she screamed for her kids when she couldn't handle me; they held me down, and started punching me alongside her."

I started crying uncontrollably. The words stitched into scenes within my head and I pictured my mother being outnumbered and beaten by a bunch of savages. It made me sad and angry. I clenched my fists, wanting to hit something and wanting to hit it hard.

Women are the only oppressed group in our society that lives in intimate association with their oppressor - I was filled with such turmoil as she continued to tell her story.

"Your father and grandmother were watching as they beat me up," our eyes grew wide then. *They watched her get beaten mercilessly? What the hell!*

"I called to them for help--looked right into your father's eyes and reminded him I was the mother of his kids. But he turned away and your grandmother looked down on me and said, "That's what you deserve, letting your girls step out of line like that." She left her house and Najwa's son took my phone."

She paused, before crying again; my heart hurt alongside her pain. "They took my phone and they broke it when you guys kept calling me. I was afraid; I tried fighting back, but it was hard; they had me pinned down. Then they called the police and framed me being there, as if I was jealous of your father's new girlfriend and went there to start trouble. I explained my end, but they didn't believe me," she sobbed. "They didn't believe me; they threatened to arrest me and pushed me outside the house."

Seeing her like this, seeing her sad like this made me see red. I was tired of Najwa ruling over the community in the shadows; I hated how she was in charge of what people said, what they did, and when they did things. I was tired of seeing the pain she continued to put Yuma through.

That's when the fire of rage burned like wildfire inside of me. It consumed me; I was no longer going to take their shit. I was no longer going to be afraid of them. I had it; this was it. I was not going to hide and shy away anymore. It was time to adopt the mentality Ilham had. She was a warrior, always willing and ready to jump into battle for the ones she loved, never caring if she were to lose a limb in the process. I hated my grandmother, I hated my father and I hated Najwa. Those hypocrites would burn and live to regret the day they ever laid their filthy, sinful hands on my mother. How dare he hurt the woman who raised his kids for him, as he lay in jail, rotting for a stupid act he committed?! How dare he not defend the woman who made others look onto our family and wish we were their children?! How dare he sit there and look down on the woman who made his shitty, pathetic life full of purpose. My skin burned with hate and revenge; Amani was no longer the silent observer. She would kick, scream and shout just as loud as our oppressors.

Livid! I was fuming with anger at how he could just sit there and watch her get beaten up. Regardless of how much you're fighting, you don't just let anyone put their hands on the woman who carried your slack for over ten years.

We were angry, scared, lost and unaware of what else to do. We convinced Yuma to let us take her to see Hasib. Gently, we helped her into the car and made sure to bandage her up properly. The sight of her in the daylight made her look so much worse. My heart squeezed in agony at our idol's state. Jumping into the car, we drove right back to the halfway house and begged the officer to see Hasib. We explained it was an emergency and he needed to see us immediately. Overwhelmed, the officer was hesitant about letting us see him.

"Please sir, it's an emergency! He needs to see our mom right now. Look at her, he needs to know what's going on. Please, it'll be really quick. We have no one else to turn to."

After seeing how desperate we were to see Hasib, the officer nodded his head and told us to take a seat, as he called Hasib back into the visiting room.

Yuma was shriveled and shaken. Seeing her in pain hurt. The fire within her was punched right out, and she did nothing but sit there and stare at the wall with a blank expression on her face. Rubbing her back, we waited; I don't know what we planned to accomplish by being here, but there was no one else we could turn to. It was them versus us and we hoped and prayed that Hasib would be our saving grace.

Hasib's face dropped once he saw the state of our mother. He rushed over to her, knelt down in front of her, and with his beautiful blue-green eyes he looked concerned; he asked us what happened.

"Your wife," is what Ilham and I both spat venomously. "She was so upset that I talked back that she decided to beat Yuma up along with your daughter and a few of your sons," Ilham finished with anger so contained, her eyebrow was twitching.

"*Laa* (No)," he gasped, eyes wide in surprise. "Where was everyone else?"

"That's the best part; they were watching. Yuma called out to Siti and Alzalim for help, but they turned their heads and let Najwa beat her up," I responded with disgust dripping from every word that I spoke. I couldn't believe this was happening. There was no way this was happening right now--that the only other person we could turn to was locked away.

Hasib held Yuma's hands then and squeezed them close to his chest, "I'm sorry. I'm so sorry this happened to you and I swear to you I'll fix this. Najwa's an animal, we both know this, but she's gotten out of control. I'll fix this I promise."

It was heartwarming to see how Hasib held my mom's hands. In another life, they would have been together. He would have treated her right; he would have treated her the way she was meant to be treated. I swear, they were the ones meant for one another and everyone knew it. In another life, he could have been my father...and I would have been honored to be his daughter.

The officer cut our time short, letting Hasib know that he was doing him a favor by even letting him be here this long. Nodding his head, Hasib stood up and kissed Ilham and I on the forehead, as he wiped our tears away.

"Don't cry habibti, don't cry. This will get fixed, I promise," he assured us.

"She's our mother Hasib, why would they hurt the only person we have on our side?" I asked, sniffling with the last remaining remnants of who I once was. Pulling a tissue out from my coat pocket, I wiped my nose and hugged him tightly. "Thank you," I whispered. I was grateful for him; he always tried to keep the peace amongst our families and he was the favorite in his family. It was impossible not to love the man; he was perfect, truly perfect. He gave Yuma a squeeze on her shoulder and whispered encouraging words before helping her up to us. We said our goodbyes then. He watched as we walked out the door and headed to our car, huddled together to protect her.

Once we finally arrived home, Yuma walked slowly up the stairs and crawled into her bed, hugging her knees. Her sobs were heard as we crept up the stairs and joined her in her room. Ilham sat to her right and I to her left. We looked over her with seriousness and love that no one else could possibly understand. Imagine seeing the person you'd give your life for in a state so humiliating that it burned you raw. It was disgraceful to witness such a thing because it reminded you of what you failed to do--of what you failed to protect. That eerie sound of her sobs echoing through the halls marked her mourning over the loss of her foundation in life. It was a reminder that would stay with me forever.

Ilham and I signed on for a new war, willingly offering ourselves up for this battle to come. I looked to my left and stared at Yuma's vanity which reflected my intense gaze. My new look finally felt like it was meant for me. No longer did I feel like a fraud. I was here, I was present, and I would defend our family alongside Ilham. We were the proud warriors against all odds. No mercy would be given.

It was times like these that tested one's character; the push and pull of good versus evil shakes the plot and shapes the story for years to come. The warrior within struggles to maintain her strong demeanor; the battleground is drawn from the tears of a struggling family, exhausted from the long days and nights of constantly being on alert and preparing for battle. Now that the war had come, our greatest treasure (Yuma's spirit) was torn from us. We were on the battlefield with no ammo, no protection, and little visibility trying to see in the murky clouds ahead. The prospects for winning didn't look good, but we'd fight anyway. We had to. Onward...to war.

CHAPTER 18

Anxiety is My Frenemy

"Courage is fear holding on a minute longer."

– George S. Patton

Being anxious throughout the day and continually on a daily basis had become natural. Looking over my shoulder or checking the aisles of a store before I walked into it had become completely natural for me as well.

Growing up, my family and I were watched, and not just our family, but everyone's family in our community. The poorer your family was or the amount of power and influence your family had factored into whether or not they'd turn a blind eye to any misconduct that occurred. My immediate family contained no money or power, because the head of the household (at the time) who was my father didn't have a respectable career or any respect for himself... or his family for that matter. Our family was a laughing point of entertainment because my father did whatever the hell he wanted and cared not of what could befall his family. He was selfish, through and through, and the more I thought about it, the more I hated him.

I didn't realize that growing up in such a stressful atmosphere altered my personality, changing the wiring of my brain so that I was no longer Amani but the product of oppression in a culture that defined what fear meant for the women in my community. And yet we were expected to deal with it, because it was "normal" for us women to be put under such pressure. What did it matter right? If it isn't a man's problem, it isn't a problem.

"Do you think this high level of anxiety and paranoia, while out in public, has anything to do with your family?" asked the psychiatrist sitting across from me.

I gazed out the window noticing early signs of spring. The grey clouds that normally cover the city of Syracuse were thinning and the sun was peeking through. A few birds were visible as they chirped and chased one another around the courtyard. I shifted my view inside the office then.

The room was silent as she awaited my response; the tissue paper I carried in my hand began to fray with the amount of fidgeting I was doing. Her office showed no signs of her personality, no photos, no color--no life. It was simply grey and white, reminding me of a hospital... ugh, I hate hospitals. But she meant well. She was there to help me, after all, so who was I to judge her room decor? I was the one with the problem...and the school's resources highly recommended I make an appointment with her. So I made the appointment and now here I was, with a shrink.

"Yea...I think they have everything to do with it. To this day, it's not over and it won't ever be over."

"That depends on the course of action you'd like to take; your life is your own Amani."

I chuckled, she was so unaware--so very unaware--which is why this situation was so much more difficult, because there never seemed to be anyone I could talk to about this who understood what I, or any other young woman in the same circumstances, was going through.

"No, you see that's where you're wrong. My life isn't my own, nor is your life your own, doctor. If God can take my soul from me in a single moment, my life isn't my own. If a man can take out a gun and shoot me as soon as I walk through your door, my life isn't my own. My life is not my own; I was raised by others, and in connection with that, a part of where my life goes is up to them."

She nodded her head in deep contemplation, writing more notes down in her notepad, "So, do you feel like you need to repay them?"

I cocked my head to the side, and stared at the corner of her wall where a single cob web lay floating in the air by the vent. "Repaying comes from guilt or the need to prove that you can afford the luxury of doing so. I was threatened by my own father, that he would take my life had I ever decided to do anything to disrupt our family *honor*. So you tell me, will I ever be finished paying my debt?" making eye contact with her now. "Hmm?"

She shifted in her seat, clearly uncomfortable with the new information, "Do you believe there is actual harm in that threat?"

I laughed, "Duh, I can't sleep, eat, walk or talk without it being approved. My peers get to travel and find themselves, find their calling in life. And what am I given, huh?" The window invited the sun's rays in now, the trees swaying to the breeze. "I'm given life, yes, but I don't get to live."

"Amani, everything I'm hearing from you right now is showing me that you meet all the criteria for PTSD, or in other words, post-traumatic stress disorder. It's affected all aspects of who you are."

"What do you mean?" I asked intrigued.

"You see, there are levels to the reaches PTSD can touch you and, in your case, it's touched you on all levels. There's the mental, the physical and the operational; the disorder has not only increased anxiety and stress on your body, but it's also rewired your brain when behaving in public. Instead of opening up and being yourself when with friends, you're more withdrawn, questioning who can hear you, who knows your family among your peers and most importantly, where is your family watching you from today. You aren't fully Amani whenever you aren't within the safe walls of your room. You're afraid of how you dress and who walks beside you; you are the type that stands in the corner at parties or just socializes because you aren't comfortable in your own skin, because how it looks is more important than what it is. "

I stared at her at that moment, letting everything sink in. PTSD huh; wow, I didn't think it was that serious but here is this paid professional breaking down my troubles and letting me know that I've watered down my personality, in fear of being expelled from my family. It was insane really, to hear that the stress my family put me under, the pressure my mom constantly reminded me of everyday had pushed and wedged itself deep into the functioning operations of how I conduct myself in public.

A quick image of Yuma's appearance after being beaten up flashed in my mind reminding me of the consequences of retaliation. Wincing, I shook the memory from my mind and tried to refocus.

I sighed and slumped into my chair, "You're right. It's so obvious when you say it, like it's been there all along yet, while I was in the thick of it I couldn't see it."

She responded with a smile, "Of course, you wouldn't be able to notice something that has been a part of you since before you operated on your own levels of alert observations. And it's not your fault."

I waved off that comment, "I'm not here for an ego stroke doc; I know it's not necessarily my fault, but I'm stuck IN this position. I can't just leave, no one leaves."

"You're choosing to stay because of your mother Amani, otherwise, you could begin the path to find who you are and restore what has been taken from you, yourself. And don't you deserve to be Amani?"

I began to wonder where the Amani I was supposed to be was hiding? Where did she sleep awaiting to be welcomed in? I finally understood the feeling I've been feeling for so long. During days where I walked across the campus feeling alone, feeling incomplete, hollow, feeling like I wasn't...there. I understood it all then. I was a doll. I looked and acted the part to which my handler wanted but I carried no personality of my own. I shed tears then, mourning the loss of my character before it even had the chance to develop. I was at a loss of words and could do nothing but silently weep for the child inside of me that just wanted to experience life without the added and unnecessary pressure.

"I don't know who Amani is or is supposed to be...I've never been able to meet her. Maybe we crossed paths in passing, like students crossing Marshal Street. Familiar, and yet, so alien. I would love to meet her someday though, wondering where the hell she's been for 20 years."

"Maybe she's the one waiting for you."

Continuing on my path to find whatever lies ahead for me, I wept. I was robbed of the one thing I needed...myself.

CHAPTER 19

Shackles

"As long as the shackles of wealth and property bind
us, we will remain accursed forever and never attain
the altar of humanity, which is life's ultimate goal."

– Munshi Premchand

I was beginning to grow more and more exhausted from all it all.
After a few years dealing with the consistent and added pressure
that our distant relatives put on us, I began to see it for what it really
was. Looking down at my hands, I saw the strains clearly on my wrists
from seemingly real chains and shackles embedded in my skin from
prolonged wear, searing their mark into my flesh. It was exhausting,
to move in ways you didn't want to move, to have to do things or say
things without your consent or concern in the matter. I grew to despise
the shackles wrapped so tightly around my neck, wrists and ankles.
Anger brewed within me as I turned to Yuma and begged her to figure
out a way for us to get out of here, to no avail. She was in a much worse
state than I.

The years of oppression and neglect our acclaimed family put her through wrought more damage on Yuma than even I could comprehend. The stress had immobilized her in more ways than the rest of us. In Yuma's case, it was as if not only her wrists, ankles and neck were shackled down, but she was also gagged and blindfolded. Her chains offered her no movement whatsoever, as she lay completely still in the one position they had chained her down to. I was terrified that I would become her, that my efforts would never counteract these shackles and thus I'd give up, becoming as tortured as she.

NO! My mind screamed against the panicked thoughts coursing its way through my brain. I couldn't allow this to happen. I couldn't remain stuck like her; I couldn't throw away any chance of happiness I had because they want me to act, be and live the way they saw fit. Rebelling, I yanked my arm from the chain causing the shackles to skid firmly across my skin. Pained, I bit my lip and continued fighting. *This wasn't the life for me, this wasn't for me! Set me free!*

Tears began to well up in my eyes as I turned to see if Ilham, Nur and Ayman were alright. The fog thickens leaving only Ilham and Yuma in sight. Where were Nur and Ayman? How come they weren't in my line of sight? Worry spread like wildfire within me as I continued to push my body past the reach of my invisible chains, now groaning in pain, as I struggled to fight against those who chained us. I was tired, with only so much energy available for my mental bank, in order to could keep my sanity, that the rest of my body was left drained.

As I checked on Ilham, dark clouds emerged, washing over her face, she didn't flinch as she sat there chained and depressed.

"Ilham move!" I screamed, "Move away from it, I don't know what it is but I have a bad feeling! Move!"

Slowly she looked up and met my tear streaked face, meeting my gaze with nothing but a blank face and sad eyes. I shook my head and began to cry,

"Please Ilham, please you have to fight it, you have to! We need to stick together, we need to remain strong together!"

Ilham wouldn't respond. A loud scream came from within me as I continued to push against the chains to demand my freedom. *This wasn't fair! We didn't ask for this lifestyle; we didn't ask to be judged constantly for years and live with anxiety and paranoia daily. Why did we have to suffer?* I pushed against the shackles and tried pulling my body from them as I continued to resist. The aura of dark clouds enveloped Ilham more and more, until only her face was visible; she watched me as I struggled but said nothing, as she was being overwhelmed with the darkness surrounding her. My fighting paused as I watched one tear fall from her eyes, eyes locked with mine; her pain was evident. Her message was clear--she was giving up and as the fog completely covered her face there were only glimpses of her gagged now.

I was angry then, as I watched her fall down the same path Yuma was on because it was a path she would not emerge from once she fell deeply in. Being so angry that my body felt encompassed in flames electrified me; I refused to be silenced. I refused to be blinded or allow my senses to forever remain dull. This was not the life I signed up for; this wasn't the family I wanted to be a part of. *Set me free, set me free!*

I yanked.

I wanted my freedom.

I yanked.

I wanted my voice.

I yanked.

I wanted my future.

I yanked.

I wanted to breathe.

I yanked.

I didn't want to end up like Yuma.

I yanked!

And then...I fell. The chains collapsed all around me as the shackles echoed their loud thud across the floor. Air rushed to the flesh scarred by the chains, the sensitive skin left behind burning. Brushing my hair from my face, I exhaled the nervous emotions from within me and stared at the scars around my wrists, my ankles, and touched the inflamed skin on my neck. I couldn't believe I broke free; couldn't believe I was actually able to give myself free reign to move. What was I going to do with my freedom now? How would I choose to use it? I've dreamt of this moment for so long, but to finally achieve it felt unnatural.

Steadily, I got up and balanced my weight on my own two feet before slowly proceeding to shuffle my way to Yuma. She was in a dark corner alone; her silence scared me, making me wonder if she was alive or not. I scanned her appearance, but something was off. Something was different from what either Ilham or I had. I slowly lifted her chained arm up and analyzed her wrists. What I noticed made me cringe in disgust and fear. Her flesh had grown over her shackles which were a part of her now; no matter how hard she fought she wouldn't be able to release herself. Her skin grew on top of the shackles, becoming one with her until all you could see was the chain dangling from them. I looked to her neck and saw the same happening there; my heart clenched at seeing her hanging there, gagged and blindfolded--her head down and motionless. It pained me to see my hero succumb to such abuse.

"Yuma," I whispered, staring at her limp body. Her breathing was barely audible, as I grasped her arm and hugged it tightly. Tears ran their course down my face while I couldn't contain the feeling that ripped through me.

"Momma," I whimpered, "please come back to me, please. I need you so much". I was met with silence. Falling back, I took a good look at her and then at Ilham who was now looking down and away from me. My heart clenched tighter; I had to get out, one of us had to get out if we are ever going to survive this. I often questioned why I had to be the strong one, why this was the ongoing narrative of my life. I didn't know if I was ready for this, if I was strong enough to carry the responsibility of freedom. I was still exhausted from the previous years of torment we were all put through, but I had to continue. And so, I ran and continued running but I knew not my destination. Pushing past the fog, I ran until it was white.

Riiiiiing

Riiiiiing

Riiiiiing

Rolling over, I snatched my phone from its position on my end table and snoozed my alarm. Slowly, I pulled myself up and realized my sheets, as well as, my body were soaked in sweat. Thinking back, I realized I was dreaming and yet, it felt so real. My mind and heart felt heavy. Looking down, I saw redness on my wrists; confused, I hurriedly rolled out of bed and looked into my mirror to see the same redness around my neck. How could a dream reach you in reality? Or was it a message about what was yet to come, a future I'd have to prepare for inevitably? A future I was afraid to meet and yet it was approaching whether I wanted it to or not.

CHAPTER 20

False Capes

"Sometimes you gotta be your own hero and save
your little heart. Because sometimes, the people
you can't live without, can live without you."

– Unknown

L ying in bed with nothing but my thoughts to keep me company, I lay there contemplating. What did one do after finding out they have PTSD? How do you even cope with that? How do you move on from that?

It made me angry to sit there and come to terms with the fact that my extended family members were so twisted and cruel that they changed what it meant to be a member of this community. They had affected the way I viewed my own culture--the way I viewed my own people. Now, whenever I saw someone who remotely resembled an Arab, I ran the other way. I was afraid; not in the sense that most of America was (because I viewed my religion as promoting peace and self-love.) This community that I lived in were not Muslims in my eyes; they were greedy, thieving and untrustworthy individuals. I was afraid for my mother, who (aside from her sister arriving a few years ago) was alone here dealing with my father's family for over 20 years.

My thoughts roamed to Yuma then, wondering how she was holding up. Ever since the incident I refused to see any of my extended family. The thought of them made me so angry that I felt my body temperature rising immediately. My cell phone buzzing in my pocket temporarily distracted me, until the caller ID notified me that it was Alzalim trying to reach me. Answering swiftly without hesitation, I brought the phone to my ear,

"What the hell do you want?!" my voice snapped.

"I heard you're living off campus with your sorority sisters," he stated smugly.

"As a matter of fact, I am"

"Give me the address where you live," he demanded.

"No, I won't. I won't do shit for you now, or ever. You're fucking dead to me, you are not my father, you're not related to me and I am disgusted to know a man like you to ever exist on this planet. Block my number, lose it, delete it. I don't care how you do it, but figure it out and get it done!" I could feel the anger seeping out of my eyes as I squeezed my phone tightly. *Who the fuck does he think he is?!!*

"Who the hell do you think you're talking to *ya sharamoota* (bitch)!"

"I'm telling you right now, I catch you near my residence, I catch you near Yuma's house: I WILL PERSONALLY CALL THE COPS MYSELF ON YOUR ASS! Test me! I dare you."

With a click of a button, the call dropped. I felt good; I felt empowered to finally stand up to him the way I so desperately wanted to before. *He messed up the minute he watched them beat her senseless.* As far as I was concerned, *burn in hell, you're now deceased in my book.*

Alzalim's mother wasn't someone I was too happy with in the moment either; she could have taken control of the situation since it was happening in her house, but she walked out. I wanted her to feel the shame I felt being a part of her bloodline, I wanted her to sense my hatred from afar because she was not deserving of my presence. I was disappointed in them. I hated hearing my last name and, from then on, refused to let it come out of anyone's mouth. I was no longer an Abdel Nour. I would carry my mother's maiden name and wear it proudly because I was of HER bloodline.

Picking up my cell, I dialed her number and waited patiently as the phone rang. Playing with the loose cotton on my bed sheets, I waited for the second ring before she picked up. These days I held my breath as I called her in fear that she may not pick up the phone. I was even more cautious now and that annoyed me. I didn't like to go anywhere, didn't like to do anything, I just wanted to hide away and never emerge, so that I wouldn't risk harm falling upon my mother again. After all, it was our fault she was beaten up in the first place and that kind of shame never leaves you...ever.

"Hello," her depressed voice filtered through the phone.

"*Asalam wa alaikum* Yuma," I said calmly.

"*Wa alaikum salam,*" she responded, "*shoe fee (what's up)?*"

"Nothing, I just wanted to check in on you and see how you're doing. How are you Yuma?"

"*Taaban* Amani (I'm tired Amani), I can't sleep anymore. My head hurts at night when I think too much."

I sighed with a heavy heart, "Aww, Yuma I'm sorry to hear that. Have you tried drinking tea or warm milk?"

"Ehhhh," she began, "that doesn't work with me, I'm taking sleeping pills to help me sleep these days."

"Yuma, you know you're going to become addicted to those soon. You can't rely on them as much as you are."

"I'm not, don't worry," she said all too quickly. Knowing her as well as I think I do, I assumed she probably got an entire cupboard full of them. She'd come a long way from relying on pills to help her mental or physical state. She knew better than to start relying on them again.

"Okay, you better, I'm trusting you with this. How's everyone at home?"

"*Koolhom la halhom* (they're all to themselves) Amani, *alla telephone ou computer* (on the phone and the computer)"

That was our family these days. We were a family, but not a family, always afraid to speak with one another in fear of what the individuals in the family might think or use as blackmail. Our lives were private to us; no one knew what the other was doing in their life nor did anyone care to know. Each of us carried the mentality, *if I don't ask about them, they won't ask about me.* It was sad; we had become so afraid of our extended family or the way things were run in this community that we would rather sit silently than say anything at all and that wasn't something I was happy to be a part of.

I hadn't checked in on my family in what seemed like years and had no idea what was currently going on in their lives. I felt bad that I wasn't doing my part as a daughter or as a sister to be there for them when they needed me most. I was determined to detach myself from my family completely and I hadn't realized it. I was just so tired of drama always following us everywhere we went when we didn't even deserve such treatment. Tons of other kids are out there doing way worse than we had ever done, and yet they are not called into the spotlight nor are their parents being lured into extended family households where they then get beat up. Why was our family consistently the target? *Oh wait... it's because we were poor and had no man to stand up for us.*

It was funny how families with single mothers were seen as weak, or people would pity a family with a woman as the head of their household. I found it shocking that people saw such families as unfortunate or weak, when it was really quite the opposite. *Yes, we are a part of a single mother household but look how strong of a single parent Yuma is.* She raised four kids all on her own; worked to feed and support us, educated us on the lessons of life and drilled into our heads that college was our guaranteed right of redemption. On her own, she carried us on her back as she learned to speak English when her husband was locked away or cheating. On her own, she figured out how to hire a driver's ed teacher, in order to learn how to drive and got herself a driver's license. It was she, alone, who taught my siblings and I what it meant to truly be a Muslim. Every night we would sit at the foot of her bed and listen to her read the Quran with her soft voice, her words as soothing as a warm bath. I sank into them, bathed in the fluid language that flowed so effortlessly from her mouth and let them consume my soul. I felt at peace then, truly happy to be in her presence, even though at that time we barely had anything to call our own.

I remember telling my mom at such a young age that it didn't matter if we had no money to call our own or any houses to claim; that as long as we had one another, that's all we'd ever need. I didn't realize it then, but thinking back on it now, I could see the happiness light up in her eyes then, even though it didn't register on her face. She always felt bad that she couldn't give us the world like many other mothers could, and that we would make toys from paper and watch the same VHS tapes over and over again without fail. But hearing those words coming from a child that barely understood a thing that was going on around her meant a lot to her. It meant her efforts were recognized and appreciated.

"I love you Yuma, so much" I fondly stated, recalling the memories of how affectionate she once was with us back when she carried hope.

"I love you too Amani. Please don't do anything wrong and be sure to watch your actions. Always keep Allah in your thoughts and know that he will always know what you do before you do them."

"I know Yuma," I responded, rolling my eyes. She never failed to text me or remind me of the same thing over the phone every day. It bothered me to be reminded daily; it translated to me like, "Just remember Najwa is watching". *Isn't she always watching?*

"You know Hasib didn't do anything. He's afraid of Najwa; she has all his business under her name and his house too. You really think he was going to stand up for us?"

I stood up then, why was I just now hearing about this? I thought the issue would have been dealt with and handled efficiently. To hear that nothing came of this, that no one was suffering the consequences of their actions made me angry.

"He didn't do anything?" I asked again for confirmation. I couldn't believe what I was hearing.

"No, he told your sister that you two should have never gotten involved in their son's business--that you two needed to learn to watch your mouths and respect your aunt."

I couldn't believe what I was hearing; there was no way I was hearing this correctly whatsoever. We trusted him; we put all of our last hopes in him, hoping that the man who always pursued good over evil would be our savior. I had no doubts with him which is why I was so confused. *Why would he let us down knowing that we were defenseless, knowing that there was no one on our side?*

The memories I had with him began to darken; no longer did I think of sunshine and bird song as his face came across my thoughts; no longer did I think he was a man of the people. He was a coward who was afraid to stand up against his wife and mother--a true coward who preached about having dreams of the future without ever actually achieving them. How can a man stress that family must always remain strong, yet fail to hold wrongdoers within his own family accountable? I couldn't wrap my head around it; none of this made sense. He wanted us to be his family, he wanted to see us happy, so why would he turn his back on us now? Was money that important? Were his businesses that important? What had our family ever done to him to make him not stand up and tell his wife that enough was enough. *Forget the great or grand gestures I dreamed you'd do, just simply tell her to back off our family.* We wanted nothing to do with the drama she presented.

It dawned on me then that he never called me; I gave him my number during our last visit and he promised he would call me, as soon as he was given the opportunity. Weeks later, I still have not received a response. I was hurt. I took it more personally than anyone else in my family, because for some odd reason, I personally idolized him. I truly thought he was an angel sent to us and to feel such a betrayal from your super hero--it was devastating. It made you question the validity of everything else. I didn't want to see him that way; I didn't want to see him as the man who cried wolf. I didn't want to...but the facts were there. I knew it was hard for Yuma to bring it up; she knew I saw him as a father and that part of the reason I worked so hard in school was also to make him proud. I loved seeing the smile on his face, loved seeing how proud he was and how his hugs told me that he was very proud of my growth and accomplishments. (I didn't know it then, but it was only a few weeks after this phone call did I happen across his number only for him to ignore my calls and messages. She got to him, made sure he never spoke to us again without her go ahead. All my attempts to remain in touch were lost on him.) Najwa had won. She had him back in her grasp--back in her realm.

Hasib how could you love a woman that betrayed your love? Do you truly believe she is deserving of your love? Your affection and time? I cannot understand why people choose to accept a binding contract as love rather than the attachment the heart strings connect with.

Hasib you were once my hero, you were once the definition of what hope and light looked like on Earth. You were a huge part in the happiness of my childhood even though I never got to see you, even though you never kept your word or fulfilled any of your promises. It's sad to me that your youngest brother, of whom looked up to you and Alzalim, always worked hard to show face in my siblings' life and mine; he always worked hard to make sure he kept his promises and that he always instilled faith in our future the way our father failed to do. Yet I never gave him the love and affirmation he deserved because I was hell bent on believing that the man who never failed to smile in our sight was going to bring us to the promised land. *I had complete faith in you and you let me down.*

Hanging up the phone with a heart as heavy as stone, I sat back down and sighed. I began to see the grey clouds in the memories I had with him now. I remembered the false promises and the sadness that enveloped me whenever he canceled plans with us. I remember looking outside yearning to see his car pull up only to turn away from the window an hour later saddened by the lack of his presence.

I cried then, not like the 20-year-old I was. I cried like the child inside of me that watched him get locked away and prayed for his release, only to come to terms with the misplaced faith in a man whom I thought was a hero. I cried knowing that I chose the wrong man to fill a hero's cape when he was just a man. And men were made imperfect.

CHAPTER 21

Eid, Time of Celebration

"In our work and in our living, we must recognize
that difference is a reason for celebration and
growth, rather than a reason for destruction."

– Audre Lorde

The week started off with bad news about Hasib. We buried a hero and it was the most depressing feeling imaginable. I never imagined I would see this day; I felt as though I was in the Twilight Zone. Things just weren't right. I didn't want to hear anything else pertaining to my family. Everything was just so messed up now, happening so fast and I had no idea how it got this way. We were doing so well at one time, where did that go?

Not being able to handle the thoughts that tortured me, I laced on my shoes, flicked off the lights to my room, locked my door and headed out. Where I was headed--I had no clue, but walking would allow my thoughts to process clearly. The street I lived on lay quiet and still at this time; the soft whistling of the wind so warm and fragile against my cheek made me smile. I embraced its touch with eyes closed, its unexpected presence making goosebumps rise out of my skin. Taking a deep breath in and remaining still, I allowed the air to enter my body and relax my constricted and tense muscles. As I exhaled, I relished in the feeling of the fog clearing my head and body.

The sound of music and laughter caught my attention; opening my eyes, I searched for the source and saw that across the street from me was a family enjoying a cookout together. Beers in hand, the smell of barbecued chicken filled the air. They huddled around one another, sharing jokes and pictures of replayed memories. I marveled at the beauty of their bond and remembered a time when my family once joined our extended relatives to celebrate important events--events like Eid.

Eid happened twice a year. The first event (Eid Al-Fitr) was a celebration of the completion of Ramadan and breaking of the fast that included 29 or 30 days of dawn to sunset fasting. The second part of Eid (Eid Al-Adha) was a celebration of Ibrahim's willingness to sacrifice his son on God's command. Before that sacrifice occurred, however, God sent his angel Gabriel to intervene by putting a sheep in place of the son, as a sacrifice. During this celebration, we sacrifice an animal in the name of God and divide it into 3 portions. The first portion is for family, the second is for friends, extended family and/or neighbors, and the last portion is given to the poor and needy. Eid Al-Adha is also a celebration of Muslim migration to Mecca and of those who decide to make the pilgrimage.

In the past, it was during the time of Eid Al-Adha that we'd head over to Siti's place from dawn until dusk. We'd wake up excited and we'd be dressed and ready before Yuma even woke up. This was the time of year that we got to see everyone, and by everyone, I mean people I had not seen in well over a few years. Yuma did a pretty good job of keeping our family away from anyone she thought had the potential to throw us into drama.

The sun always shines on days like this. It seemed that God would bless us with beautiful days during this time of the year. Yuma would wake up and see the excitement on our faces; skipping her morning coffee, she rushed herself just so we could head to Siti's earlier. We dressed in our finest; it was always a time to dress your best because those who did not see you in a while were curious to see what had become of you.

I was always nervous, given that I didn't really blend well with my family much. Ilham always loved these functions because she loved everything that had to do with our family. She loved the jokes, the conversations, the never-ending weddings and house visits. Always trying to go to someone's house alongside Siti, she was what many of my extended family wished I could also be. But I was more like Yuma, more reserved, and kept away from everyone. I knew that no matter how friendly they acted, they only did so to gather information on us to tell the rest of the community in their own twisted version of the facts. Usually, they would hype their stories to get people probing or asking more questions.

In the car, we blasted the music and sang along with the artist, named Abdel Halim Hafez, that Yuma loved since she was a young girl. Whenever she played his music we knew she was in a good or relaxed mood. She played him on her good days and Eid was always a good day. On the days his deep and calm voice filled the car, you would hear and see Yuma singing along, which was a rare sight in itself. She felt for him, saying he was a true gentleman and not many boys were raised to be like him these days. His music touched her soul with his pain-filled voice and life experiences. In many ways, I believe he aided in soothing her pain, for the way she sang along, it mirrored the suffering in his own voice.

Turning onto the street that Siti lived on, the excitement in the car grew. Siti's house stood tall and grand on the corner of her street. The focal point of her block, she ruled the area and everyone knew it. Her backyard was so big, it wrapped all the way around her house and was paradise to kids my age. Everyone in the neighborhood knew who she was and made it a point to show their faces whenever they could out of respect for her.

Hopping out of the car, we raced one another to the porch and bombarded her foyer before she even had the chance to take a glance outside. Pushing and pulling one another, our giggles were heard long before we became visible.

"Siti!!" we all called, excited as little kids can get. We each greeted her respectively before Yuma came in and gave her simple, yet respectful greeting. Siti asked how the prison visit went with Alzalim, and as Yuma informed her, we snuck into the guest room to see all the sweets she had laid out for her guests to enjoy whenever they stopped by for a visit. Pistachio cookies, baklava, and date cookies were all before us!

"Rruhum min salown (Get out of the room)!" she'd call out in Arabic. "Intomb mish adyuff (You guys aren't guests)! Let them have some first and then you guys can!"

Giggling, we grabbed a handful of candy before stuffing it in our pants and shouting, "Okay Siti, we're leaving!" Running to the kid's guest room, we jumped on the couch and played with the candy wrappers we just unraveled. We rolled them in balls and threw them across the room at each other while chewing the sweet candy on our tongues.

"How much money do you think we're going to get?" Ayman asked eager to buy more video games.

"I don't know, maybe a lot. What do you think Ilham?" I asked looking to her; she always knew everything, and as much as it annoyed me, it was super beneficial at times.

"Well the most we've ever gotten from one person is $20 dollars, so it really depends on how many people come by. I'd say maybe about $100, easy."

Ayman and I lit up with excitement, as $100 was more than you could imagine for us as kids. Our eagerness only grew then; no more paper made toys for us whenever Eid rolled around--hard plastic, here we come!

During the celebration of Eid, kids and women were always given money and/or gifts. It was the equivalent of Christmas to us and boy did we feel lucky to have it twice a year. The mornings were always slow at Siti's during Eid, because everyone was at prayer--it was a traditional thing to complete Salat El Eid (Eid prayer) to start the day off right. Towards the afternoon is when cars started pulling up to the house, which caused squeals of joy to come out of our mouths.

"Go in the other room and sit down appropriately, especially you and Ilham," Yuma requested.

"Okay, Yuma," I responded nodding my head before relaying the message to Ilham. We re-entered the children's guest room and sat down quietly. Once the first guests arrived, there would be no stopping the stream of ongoing visitors and then the fun would truly begin. Bringing funny stories with them, the guests filled the air with laughter and the smell of Turkish coffee would float in and out of the rooms. Everyone's voices would rise and the house would carry about four or five different conversations at one time. Festive music played in the background while cigarette smoke floated out into the windows and alerted us that grown men were on the porch discussing business.

Recalling the memory made me yearn for such beautiful moments again. Everyone was happy then, and life was drama-free from what I could recall as a kid. As children, we paid no mind to the conversations going on in the next room. We were only focused on the kids that would file in as their parents came and then dispersed once it was time to go. We'd run across the house and around the backyard where there were a few games of soccer or football going on. The music would be playing loudly, and the festivities never seemed to end; to me, these moments represented the true definition of family gatherings. If anyone ever wondered what family looked or felt like, I would say, "right here, look right here and this is what family looks like."

But thinking back to those times now and reliving those memories made me see things I had not previously noticed. There was one woman who attended Eid at Siti's household, by the name of Lucida. She was the mother of three daughters who decided that they would rather live their lives then deal with the burden of our culture, or rather, the way our family misconstrues the beauty of our culture. And because of their actions, Lucida was looked upon with disgrace and dishonor. No one respected her and whenever she did come around there were always whispers being spoken of her inability to raise her children or keep them in line without their father around. Such whispers caused her reputation to hit rock bottom, even though she was a very religious woman. Her nature did not make up for her daughters' behavior in the eyes of the community I lived in.

I contemplated the audacity of such a thing: *how can she be good in the eyes of God, but not for those in our community?* I shook my head at such a thought. She couldn't save her reputation no matter what she did afterwards. No matter how religious she was, they found all sorts of excuses to denounce Lucida: "She's only praying because her daughters are sluts." It made me angry to hear such thoughts because she was, in fact, a kind woman.

Upon seeing her, I got up to go greet her the way we were supposed to, but found myself intercepted by Yuma. "Go sit down Amani; we don't greet her. She isn't good enough to be greeted by someone as pure as you."

I was confused when I was younger, but being as old as I am now I understood. The sins of her children carried over to Lucida; their sins became hers and the consequences they hold, the parents hold as well. In the eyes of God, however, we are able to be forgiven. In Islam we can save ourselves from the sins of our past, but the way this family of mine picked and chose which parts of the religion they'd keep and follow, compared to what they'd rather pull from their own political agenda, was mind blowing to me. No one should insert cultural practices into the Quran to create a whole new norm. The Quran preaches peace and acceptance for everyone, so why is it that other human beings who make just as many mistakes, cannot find it in themselves to forgive such actions as her daughters' and pray for them instead? What is the point of claiming Islam as your religion when you don't even pray for your fellow sisters? There is no honor in shunning those that did not end up making the "right" decisions. But of course, they'd suppress my opinion because I "didn't know better" as a child.

"But Yuma why? She didn't do anything," I asked confused. Lucida looked kind with a marvelous smile on her face, as she attempted to greet everyone in the room that went silent. She felt the tension in the room and knew the drop in enthusiasm was because of her arrival. God bless her soul, she pretended not to notice. Her smile a bit shaken and her hands clenched by her side, she nodded to everyone without doing the traditional and customary kiss on the cheek or handshake.

"Hello everyone, may peace be upon you. I wanted to stop by and wish everyone a wonderful Eid and may God watch over your families," she politely announced.

The room was still awkwardly quiet before Siti cleared her throat and responded without fail, "We thank you for your wishes and hope the same for you and your girls, may they keep God in their hearts."

Back then, I thought that was kind of my grandmother to say, but thinking back on it now I realized it was a shot to Lucida's motherly skills--a reminder that no one respected her because of her inability to keep her daughters virgins. She shied away then, saying her goodbye and then out the door she went. I remember watching her leave, as the laughter picked up then, the music being played louder and the festivities continuing as if they never paused.

Watching her car pull out, I made eye contact with her; she gave me a slight smile to which I smiled back wholeheartedly. She didn't do anything wrong to me, she was always a kind woman. I would not judge her the way others did when she meant no harm to any of us.

Waving to her I called out, "Goodbye! Have a happy and beautiful Eid!"

She laughed then before honking once and pulling into the busy streets, filled with kids kicking soccer balls around and riding bicycles. I jumped onto the bench on the porch and stared at her car ride all the way down the street until it turned the corner and out of sight--out of the zone of judgement. I would later realize she was blessed to have escaped early on .

Judgement followed many, even on the celebration of holidays, such as these. One year in particular, during my senior year of high school--to be exact--was the groundbreaking year that Yuma dared to step out of her shell and into the den of lions. It was the year she decided that enough was enough; that year she decided that she would not be a follower of other people because of hearsay. It was the day she first stepped out in rebellion to the members within our community. That day marked the beginning of Yuma finding her voice, which laid the groundwork for her becoming the woman she needed to become to save herself.

Today marked the first Eid we would spend with Alzalim since he'd moved back in with us. I've come to learn not to expect much since we stopped celebrating as a family a while ago. These days we just considered it another holiday to spend indoors doing nothing.

Hearing his throat clear as he slowly made his way down the stairs made me cringe. I rolled my eyes before he turned the corner to face me.

"You ready?" he asked staring at me, although I clearly was unaware of any plans.

"For?" I asked with a hint of attitude.

"We're going to your grandmother's, it's Eid," he answered me in a matter of fact way.

"We never do anything though; since when do we celebrate?"

"Since we're back together as a family now." I stared at him then, wondering when he'd wanted his family back together or anything to do with us. He made it quite clear years ago that being a part of a family was not for him. That he didn't want to be tied down by us or to us. Where was this sudden change coming from?

"Okay," was all I could respond. Getting up off the couch, I headed upstairs and got dressed as Ilham finished putting on her hijab.

"Since when do we celebrate? With him?"

Ilham shrugged her shoulders, "I don't care what his reasons are, I'm just glad we're actually celebrating again."

I nodded my head in agreement; she was right. At least Nur would get to celebrate like kids should. Ilham and I worried that she was being exposed to too much sadness and violence these days with all the drama that's been surrounding the family. I feared she'd grow up more screwed up than we were. Given that Ilham had practically raised Nur, I knew she felt the same way, so she'd make sure that Nur would have a good time. We even managed to get Ayman out of his room for once to join in the festivities.

Once we were all finished, we filed down the stairs in a single line--the air filled with our various perfumes and colognes, setting the mood for the day. Yuma came downstairs with her bag, keys and shoes in hand ready to join us, but there was only one issue.

"*Yuma, your hijab,*" *Ilham pointed out. We all stared at Yuma with her straightened, black hair glistening with the oils she used to create such a shine.*

"*What about it?*" *she asked.*

I shifted forward as she joined us in the foyer, "*Well uh,*" *I began scratching my head (hijab intact),* "*it seems to be missing from your head is what this is about.*"

She continued to place her shoes on her feet, as we all followed her onto the porch confused as to what was going on. Was she not going to wear her hijab? Was she actually going to be the only woman in the family not wearing her hijab in public? What was going through her mind? Why did she decide to do this now? Did she understand what it would mean for her reputation or how it would make our family look. How was Alzalim going to react to this?

"*I know that it's not on my head, don't be rash. I'm not wearing it--not today, not tomorrow--I will no longer be wearing it.*"

All three of us stood at a loss for words; Nur continued playing outside. I couldn't wrap my head around this and couldn't bring myself to fathom the amount of scrutiny she was going to be placing on our household. She made this decision knowing full well what would happen once she stepped out in public and was spotted by anyone within the Arab community. The rumors that would be spread and the anger unleashed by Siti as we walked into her home would be the first repercussions. This would quite literally mean social suicide if Yuma decided to go through with not wearing the hijab.

"*Yuma this isn't a smart decision, you know that right? Especially, given that Ilham and I are wearing hijabs and you aren't. That'll just make you worse in comparison.*"

She glared at me then, her stare showing no fear, "There are many other things to fear in this life, than simply fearing the opinions of others Amani."

I rolled my eyes at her then; the irony was real coming from the person whose sole concern was the opinions of others. She stood tall then, walking through the front door and into the car that Alzalim was waiting in. He didn't seem to notice the stand she was taking against the community he thrived in. Not until the door slammed and she was right beside him with her perfume wafting through the atmosphere of the vehicle.

Staring at her with eyes filled with confusion, he nudged her before asking: "What in the world are you thinking going out like this?! Are you insane?!"

She glared at him with a look so fierce that it pierced the tension mounting in the car, "What's it to you what I do; you expect me to sit silently as you parade around with your numerous whores right? This is something you're going to accept."

Outraged, he removed the key from the ignition causing the rumbling of the car to come to a stop. The four of us bounced glances off the two of them, wondering what was going to happen now that Alzalim decided we weren't going anywhere.

"I will not take part in this; who do you think you are just waltzing around like you're not the mother of these kids! Have some respect for the name you carry!"

Yuma's chest puffed up as if squaring up for battle, "You have the audacity to question my behavior and yet your behavior is completely acceptable?! Get back in your place before you embarrass yourself further than you already have!"

He leaned into Yuma then, eyes locked with hers; both of them were fuming with anger and hatred for the other. The silence went on for what felt like hours before Alzalim opened his door and stepped out of the vehicle.

"I'm not going then; if you want to go against what we believe in, I won't take any part in it. You can deal with my mother yourself!"

Yuma shrugged and moved herself into the driver's seat. Shocked, we all stared at her while she shifted the car into drive and turned onto the oncoming traffic.

We couldn't believe she was going to do this--the thought itself was incomprehensible. She was literally going to brave the lion's den on the day that everyone gathered by the proverbial water hole to feast. The courage needed to do something of that magnitude was immense. I wondered then what had gone through Yuma's mind--what had made her decide to do this. What had pushed her? What had given her the courage, when she normally lacked the courage to stand up for herself and her self-respect? What was she hoping to prove by foregoing the hijab?

I watched her from the backseat, as she softly sang along to Fadel Shaker and tapped her finger on the wheel. Nur and Ilham were singing along while Ayman sat in the front--headphones on, focusing intently on his phone. Her actions didn't seem to faze anyone else now, but I was worried--was Yuma prepared to meet her fate when she arrived at Siti's? Or was she pushing her luck, pushed by the insanity she endured, being the wife of such a man as Alzalim.

Not wearing the hijab was something immensely frowned upon in our community. Given that her daughters were still in hijabs, and she wasn't, sent the wrong message to the rest of our family. In doing so, her actions would put the reputation of my siblings and I in jeopardy. The community would question whether we were being raised right or if we would be tempted to stray from our morals and tradition to live a care-free "American" lifestyle instead. Rumors might even start to spread about whether Yuma was sleeping with someone, if she was an unfit wife or unfit

mother, or even insane. Of course, no one would outwardly blame Alazim
for anything because he was "a man", and no blame would ever befall him
publicly, due to his gender.

It would only take one person to start gossiping for a chain of damage
to occur that would take months to fix. Even so, Yuma was unperturbed
as she turned into Pine Nut Street.

Taking deep breaths, we all exited the car and followed behind Yuma
as her thick black hair flowed in the wind. Siti wasn't outside on her porch
as we walked up to her home, which saved us some public humiliation
from her hollering questions. But as soon as we walked through the front
door of the buzzing household, all heads turned to watch as Yuma walked
up to Siti, head held high, and greeted her.

Siti stood back, shocked for a brief moment, before furrowing her eye-
brows and staring disapprovingly at her: "And what possessed you to walk
outside without your hijab?"

"I just felt like it; I don't want to wear it anymore. Why should it
concern you? It's not like the religion is practiced here anyways. You guys
all pray to impress one another, not God. You aren't fooling Him nor
one another."

"How dare you come in here with accusations like that?! Respect the
household you walk into; respect the dignity of your children. How your
daughters are wearing the hijab and you aren't is an outrage!" She grabbed
Yuma's arm and pulled her into the kitchen, "And in front of everyone like
that! What in God's name are you thinking! Your daughters are supposed
to act like this, not you!"

Ilham and I glanced at one another, honestly admitting to ourselves
that we had no idea what came over Yuma either. It was the question of
the hour that was on everyone's mind--why now? And why today of all
days? Was it her coming out show...a way to let everyone know all at once
that she would no longer be wearing her hijab?

The thudding of my head cautioned me that a migraine was on its way.

"I do not need to explain my actions to anyone but Allah himself. You have no right to pass judgement on me."

"Would you stop being stupid!" Siti's voice angrily called out with her gold tooth catching the light. "What will the people say huh? Do you want them to question the purity of your children?"

Yuma looked at us then, a little less confident than she was earlier. Our eyes were wide with confusion as we struggled to take in the conversation. We locked eyes for a moment--here was the woman I worshipped, standing bravely against the evil she had endured since her arrival here. Could she feel my undying love for her? Could she feel that I would hop right into battle for her? I'd do anything for her...anything at all.

Turning her gaze back to Siti, she held her head back up again, "If anyone's actions would taint the image of my children it would be your son and the whores you allow him to sleep with. I respect my marriage; I do not go sleeping around with other men or bring drugs into our home where Nur is running around. Have YOU no shame in controlling your son?"

Siti's face grew red, "AND HOW AM I SUPPOSED TO CONTROL YOUR HUSBAND?! HUH?! IF YOU DIDN'T DRIVE HIM INSANE, HE'D BE LOYAL AND DEDICATED TO YOUR HOME."

Yuma's eyes grew wide with shock and anger, "Insane?! And what about when you sold the house I bought with the last bit of my gold! What about when he ruined my credit and I had to file for bankruptcy?! When he registered for credit cards under MY NAME and used them to spend on the whores he takes with him to these vacations of his?!!" Yuma's eyes pooled with tears, "NOT ONCE! NOT ONCE DID HE TAKE ME ON A VACATION! I've been his wife since I was 19; I'm 42 now and I haven't seen this country!! I've done nothing but love him and tried to raise him where you failed him, but I can't fix a man that's been raised all his life to do shady business like you! Allah Yusa'amah (May God forgive you-sarcastically used)!"

Yuma turned to us then, eyes still pooling with tears, "Let's go, we're leaving," she ordered, already out of the door. Ilham was sad to go, given her loyalty lied with Siti. The guests didn't try to hide the fact that they were listening the entire time. They watched as we put our shoes back on. We said our goodbyes and followed behind Yuma. She was already in the car fuming to Khalto about what occurred. I knew we were headed to Khalto's home next, which I didn't mind because she was amazing, and it also helped that Khalto was my favorite aunt.

As we drove away, I couldn't help but feel tremendously proud of Yuma. She did it--although she came out crying, she wasn't defeated. She finally spoke her mind and did what she wanted, rather than what she was told to do. She was better than them, ten times over, and yet she always received the short end of the stick. It wasn't fair, and she was finally standing her ground.

Although we may not have been able to celebrate Eid the way we traditionally did, there was now a new cause for celebration. I smiled because if you looked close enough, right in the center of Yuma's back you could see it: her wings were beginning to sprout and one day she was going to break free and fly. Indeed, it was a time to celebrate. Seeing Yuma's tears roll down her cheeks as she maneuvered the streets, I could tell she was blind to it right now, which made it all the more exciting.

She was going to fly.

CHAPTER 22

The Creator and The Created

"My religion consists of a humble admiration of the illimitable
superior spirit who reveals himself in the slight details we
are able to perceive with our frail and feeble mind."

– Albert Einstein

Walking down the street, the air brushed past me without an
excuse me following the rustling of my clothes. I saw the masjid come into view and my heart felt heavy looking at the place that
I attended as a loyal worshiper. I used to pray 5 times a day with my
siblings, but as we got older and life dealt us more challenges, I felt my
religion fading away from me. I felt like a terrible Muslim because I no
longer prayed to Allah or wore a headscarf; everything I was basically
doing was a sin. Hearing the beautiful words of the Quran being spoken
made me feel guilty, because I know that God would always accept me
with open arms if my heart was in it. But I knew that I'd let Him down
again and so, I vowed not to get my hopes up about being the Muslim
woman I wanted to be, unless I was sure I could put my full heart into

it. Otherwise, I'd be fooling myself because God already knew what was in my heart; there was no point in cheating myself.

Don't get me wrong, it's not like I don't believe in my religion because I definitely do. I just...I don't know, to be honest. There was no excuse for my lack of dedication and commitment to the one being who is always there for me. Wiping my clammy hands against my pant leg, I took a deep breath--my heart quickened at the thought of entering a masjid when I had not been in one in so long. I didn't know who I would run into or what I'd say if I did run into anyone. Biting my tongue, I turned to the back of the masjid where women were instructed to enter and found my way to the balcony where women prayed. Sitting there within the silence I closed my eyes and breathed in the smell of books--the book stands were filled from head to toe with the Quran and *hadiths* from the Prophet, (SAWS - Salla Allahu 'Alaihi Wa Sallam *May the Blessing and the Peace of Allah be upon him*) which in a beautiful way, made me feel safe for once.

"*Salam wa alaikum sister*" called the *sheikh* (similar to a pastor in a church) from the balcony below.

I leaned forward. "*Wa alaikum salam sheikh,*" I responded hesitantly.

"What brings you to the house of Allah? *Sulah* has not begun yet."

"Oh no, I'm not here for prayer. I haven't been to a *masjid* in a while, so I wanted to relive the feeling of being here. I must admit, I feel like a bad Muslim," I responded admittedly, leaning my shoulders against the balcony rail.

"There is no such thing as a bad Muslim; if you have enough guilt in your heart to come and sit here today, you are not a bad Muslim. Allah is reaching out to you; he's protecting his creation from the temptations of the world."

"It's not the world I'm escaping from, it's the Arab community here."

"What troubles you?" he asked concerned. Closing the Quran he held in hand, he sat on the steps to the front stage and motioned for me to proceed.

"Brother, I would like to know: Does the religion shun those who make a mistake?" I asked, thinking of Lucida.

"Allah (SWT - Subhanahu wa ta'ala *May He be glorified and exalted*) says, 'Say; O, my servants who have transgressed against their souls! Despair not of the Mercy of Allah, for Allah forgives all sins, for he is oft-forgiving, most merciful!' You can find that in *Surah al-Zumar*. Allah does not turn away from his servants, he does not forget those who repent to him, for he is all forgiving in nature."

"Then why is it that Allah can forgive the sins of a sinner, but the people here cannot?"

"That is between them and Allah, sister; we cannot speak on their actions. 'And when you speak, then be just, though it be (against) a relative!' from *Surah Al-An Am*. They will judge, and you will find many who will judge you or those you know, but you must be aware that only Allah is worthy of judging you. We are all made from the sin of our ancestors, in that we are born sinners praying for redemption. We have no right to judge others."

"But why is it hard?"

"I'm sorry you must clarify," he asked confused.

I sighed, "The family I'm a part of and the community of Arabs make it hard to want to be a Muslim. I know it's bad for me to say, but they make everything hard. There's so many rules that's hard for me to follow. I'm always being watched and everything I do can harm my mom, and heaven--"

"Is beneath the feet of thy mother," he finished nodding his head, "what confuses you?"

"Is it true that my mom cannot get a divorce from my dad? That she must remain oppressed because the religion doesn't allow women to divorce?"

His eyebrows furrowed in confusion, "Divorce is allowed within reason; may I ask the status of their marriage?"

"They currently live together but he hits her, cheats on her, he keeps drugs in the house, and we have a baby sister. My mom can barely look at him without wanting to expel in disgust." I couldn't help but hear the revulsion in my voice as well, I hated him. More than anything.

"There are numerous reasons you've given that will allow your mother to divorce in the eyes of Allah and Islam. Who told you that you cannot divorce?"

"Siti; she said that the religion forbids it."

"That is not true. She is spreading false knowledge about the inner workings of the religion. Be careful what you hear that you may take into your heart, for many times it is for the benefit of the other."

"But if I don't listen, I'll get engaged, sent away, or oppressed because they think I'm a wild card and need taming before I got the chance to let go, as they would put it."

"Who told you this?"

"My father; he always threatened to get my older sister and I married off, but we don't want to. He tried once we graduated high school, but my older sister fought for us to get an education. He said he was allowed to do whatever he wanted, since he was our father and the religion stated he could give us in marriage to another."

"That is not true, unless the arrangement is agreed upon by both the soon to be bride and groom; the very idea is null. A woman should not be forced into a marriage she did not consent to."

"Then why do they keep saying the religion says they can?" I asked frustrated and clearly confused.

"It seems they are using similar ideas from the Quran and molding them into much more extreme and constricting measures to control your family. Allah (SAWS) does not condone such violence onto oneself or onto others. Our beautiful religion is one of peace; we must treat those around us as if they were our brothers and sisters because, as Allah's creations, we are all siblings."

I sat there bewildered at the thought that certain relatives were using parts of the religion and parts of our culture to construct their own society where their rules are in full effect. Taking innocent children and allowing them to believe that their rules growing up were the actual religion or the way our culture was supposed to be. But it wasn't, and not all of us knew that. We were conditioned at such a young age to buy into the society they falsely created--a community based off a hierarchy that would remain in power and never allow one to move up the ladder. It angered me to know this, considering I started to dislike my religion or my culture thinking it just wasn't for me because of this pseudo-community which was not even based on our genuine culture or my faith. Our community practices were being controlled by a bunch of twisted individuals who thought they knew best for us, when really they did so out of greed for power.

This life I was living was not my religion's fault.

This life I was living was not my culture's fault.

My relatives were just as much the victims as I was, being taken for granted, used and torn apart until they were no longer of use. I was shocked; their actions had made me hide in fear and had influenced my personality to change completely. The damage had been done and there was nothing more I could do about that. I shrank in my chair, shocked that I was now the Muslim woman I didn't want to be; I'd always wanted to remain a faithful servant of God, but the actions of my family and what I was made to believe as a child growing up until now made me want to run from anything and anyone that reminded me of them...and sadly, my religion had become one of those reminders.

"Brother, I am not worthy of forgiveness; this I know. I have not been a good Muslim at all, to the point where I consciously know I am not good, but I don't care anymore. I'm tired, so tired."

"We all have committed sins in our life; we have all done things that we are not proud of. We are all born to eventually take part in sin, but that is what makes Allah so great--he is merciful. He understands that he made us imperfect, even the prophets had their faults, sister. Do not say you are unworthy of Allah's forgiveness. In Islam, all sins can be washed away if you turn to him and pray. Pray sister; let him feel what is in your heart--the agony you and your family are going through. Those who have been listening to *Shatan* (the devil) will get their punishment in time from Allah, it is not for us to decide."

I cried then, weeping in my lap as the recitation of the Quran floated in the atmosphere surrounding me.

Bismillaah ar-Rahman ar-Raheem (In the name of Allah, the most Gracious, the most Merciful).

He was right, all I needed to do was pray; pray to the Highest and beg him to guide me through this time--to guide my mother, my sisters and my brother. We needed His help. We needed a sign of hope that things would get better. Anything was better than the life we were living right now...anything. We had given up on Him too quickly; we'd given up on His guidance too soon, when He had only just begun showing us what he could do for us. I cried for the life we lost; I cried for the strength we gained in having one another to bring us through these times; I cried for the fear of tomorrow and the unknown that would come with it.

Aameen (Amen).

How could any woman in my position release the frustration of what we were going through? How could I explain the fear of stepping on the wrong foot? The pressures and stress we carry? How one action could tear down years of honor and pride a family name carried. We were expected to be perfect and, to me, that was the most stressful requirement of the bunch--if we were not made perfect, then how were we expected to act in such an impeccable way? It made no sense and yet, to this community, it was as if it was provided to us by nature. No wonder Yuma hid; no wonder she pulled us away from all of them. She was afraid--afraid that one small action we did would cause our entire family to come tumbling down. She hid, not because she wanted to just get away from everyone as she claimed. She hid because she was afraid. Many women in our position were afraid too. I began to carry the stress, responsibilities and fear that Yuma did. And that worried me, as well. *Fear the prayer of the oppressed.*

CHAPTER 23

Unmarked Graves

"Do not judge the bereaved mother. She comes in many
forms. She is breathing but she is dying. She may look
young, but inside she has become ancient. She smiles
but her heart sobs. She walks, she talks, she cooks, she
cleans, she works, she is but she is not, all at once. She
is here but part of her is elsewhere for eternity."

– Unknown

Leaving the mosque, I felt somewhat lighter, as if some kind of burden was lifted and taken from me. I knew now that it was never
too late to do better, be better, or become better for myself. I was the
captain of my ship; the master of my fate, and the future was unwritten.
Standing outside the mosque, I felt calm and my soul felt at peace--it felt
good. Looking across the street, I noticed our family graveyard; we had
an entire section to ourselves and although small, it contained members
of our family history who now rested eternally in peace. Crossing the
street, I let the wind push me forward and into the taboo graveyard that
was forbidden; it was forbidden for women to enter a graveyard because
of what is regarded as our attachment to the dead: our emotions are

heightened and with that came immeasurable pain. To protect us, Allah (SWT) had ordered that women were no longer allowed to visit the graveyard. But I had never seen our family who lay beneath the soil; I felt I needed to see them just once.

I crouched down to see the marked grave of my grandfather, Ayman, on my father's side. Touching the stone, I wondered if I'd feel any connection to him. Apparently, he'd passed away before I was born and so I never got to meet the man that raised Alzalim. I always wondered what kind of man he was, how he treated others or what lessons he tried to instill in his children.

Alzalim was more like Yuma than he wanted to admit; he too, never spoke about his past or his experiences growing up. These actions left us a legacy full of mystery, rather than history with us. He spoke in riddles about his past and never delved into details, which, always annoyed me. Why did they want to keep their past a secret so badly? It couldn't have been that useful to know such information so why hide it?

The mere thought that, beneath the ground, I was standing on was the skeleton of a man who once lived and breathed on this very earth unnerved me. An entire graveyard of deceased personalities and stories that may or may not have been told. Scanning the field before me, I stood there astonished. Yuma once told me that one of the prophets mentioned in the Quran would come to the graveyard every day to remind himself of where we would all end up one day. None of the material things in life mattered because at the end of the day, we were all wiped off the earth and placed beneath the ground with nothing but a coffin and some tears of our loved ones to keep us company. It scared me; I wasn't sure if I was ready to die and meet God with the list of my sins. I had far too many to count these days.

Walking on ahead, I decide to take a look at the gravestones that littered the land. Reading over the tombstones, I smiled at many of the kind words people used to describe the deceased. It was truly beautiful. Coming across one grave stopped me in my tracks, as such a tombstone would make anyone want to weep in its wake. It was small, very small, and engraved on the headstone was a baby, smiling so innocently. To die a few months after one's birth made anyone's problems seem unimportant. Losing an innocent life really changes the entire dynamic of a family. Life seems harsh and unfair, the Grim Reaper being abhorred as it carried the soul away and far from the loving arms of their mother.

I sat down in front of the grave; sighing, I introduced myself but continued, "I know this is weird, but I wanted to drop by and say a few things. Maybe you can hear me, maybe you can't, but regardless I hope you do."

Picking up shreds of grass, I began flicking them one by one before continuing, "I know you may have thought that since you died at 5 months you could have easily been forgotten because you weren't around long enough to make your mark. But that's not true. Someone I knew once lost a baby; they lost it right before the baby was born too. During that time no one understood why she locked herself away in her room all the time--why she cried randomly or stopped eating all together. She was a mess and quite frankly we were all afraid she'd die.

You see it wasn't until about a year later that I learned she'd had an abortion and since then, despised herself for removing her own child from within her. During the time in which she found out she was pregnant she was separated from her husband. Afraid she wouldn't be able to make enough money to sustain the growth and wellbeing of yet another child when she already had four, she decided that it was best to remove it and allow God to take the reins on this one.

But she wasn't the same; sleeping all night and crying all day, losing her baby by choice rather than fate destroyed her. She cradled her stomach every day in bed, prayed to God to be forgiven for the sin she had committed, and hoped her deceased child was taken care of. It changed her forever. It changed the way she treated her other children. Handling them with more love and affection, she began asking them how they were and joined them for dinner rather than seeking the dark confines of her room. The day she severed her bond with her fetus she lost a piece of herself. It hovered beside her, consumed her thoughts and eventually took a piece of her to their grave."

The last of the grass shards were picked up by the wind and rode along the wind current to its next destination. My gaze watched along as they floated out of sight and then I turned my attention back to the grave,

"My point is that although you were taken away from the world so early, you are never forgotten. You left a wide gaping hole in your mother's heart as well as your family's. The death of the innocent always remains with us--no matter how much time or distance separate us. There's a connection that cannot be broken. I promise you that."

Looking up I scanned the graves displayed out in front of me: They were of all shapes, sizes, ages and looks. Death had held no specific requirement for age or design. It had taken all forms of life--human and animal alike. None would be strangers to its call..

I sat there remembering the look of grief on her face...the sadness that exploded in her whenever it was mentioned. How the pain never faded but remained within her--a memory of what was lost. I remember the day I found out about the brother I would never know. The brother I would never meet was long gone--the brother that Ayman would never have to guide and teach, in his footsteps. My heart grew heavy and saddened by the fact that our brother was taken away from us because Yuma was incapable of feeding another mouth and raising another child while she was separated from Alzalim. Which of these graves would have been his? Was he even here? Did he have a name and if so, what was it? How small was he when he was aborted?

I was sad for Nur mostly; she would grow up without siblings to play with because the rest of us were in college figuring out the rest of our lives. This little boy would have been her partner in crime in all her adventures; he would have been someone she could teach, care for and never feel alone beside.

The burden of choice was a cruel burden to bear, when you think about never fully knowing the alternate outcomes, but have to make that choice anyway. It's scary, really, to make choices now that can potentially affect us in the moment, tomorrow or even years from now. These choices weren't temporary; they remained like the stain of wine on white clothing. They left their mark, never rubbing off or fading.

Our unborn brother was buried somewhere in this world, waiting to be visited by the family he was supposed to belong to. He was waiting out there, to be loved and pleaded with for forgiveness. He was waiting for a family that would never show.

Gripping the ground, I lifted myself up, and dusted myself off. Inhaling softly, I shook my head at the unfortunate events within Yuma's life. Would it never end? Was she doomed to struggle her entire life?

A mother is not without love for her children, however deeply buried that love is. She will always have the primal instinct to protect that of which are her own. There are times where I still catch her, hand on stomach, praying softly for God to forgive her....and then softly, in a whisper barely audible...she asks my unborn baby brother for forgiveness wherever his unmarked grave lay.

CHAPTER 24

Invisible Bookends

"Turn your wounds into wisdom."

– Oprah Winfrey

I awoke to screaming with the sound vibrating the walls of the house. Ilham and Yuma were in a screaming match again, probably about something Ilham said that she probably should have kept in her thoughts. I sighed, turning over in my bed and hoping for it to stop soon. I didn't want to wake up yet; I didn't want to face another day filled with drama and unexpected visits from people I would be fine in never seeing again.

"You always do this! You have to see that there is a time and place to say things and that isn't the time to say it!" Yuma yelled with her broken English.

"I don't care! He always does stuff like this and he never gets shit for it! But I do?! How does that make sense?!" She retorted angrily.

I moaned annoyed. Nope, this was just starting and it showed no signs of stopping anytime soon. Regrettably, I got up and looked out the window of the room Ilham and I shared. The sun was out and blazing. Birds were chirping and chattering away--one fluttered across to other trees as others flapped their wings and flew into the distance. I watched as one particular bird flew high above the rest, soaring ever so softly as the wind picked it up and traveled alongside it for company. They were free, unchained, and unbothered by the turmoil going on beneath them. It was just them and the sky, blue and open.

SLAM.

I jumped and turned to face the door. Ilham had entered the room angry and disturbed. I wanted to ask what was wrong, but then I realized I didn't care, I wanted no opinion on the matter, and wanted no knowledge of whatever had gone on between them. It was between her and Yuma and any discussion about it to me would involve me.

"I'm so angry," she threw into the air. I knew this was Ilham's way of initiating conversation about this with me. I could feel her gaze on my back, as I stared at my reflection. Damn it.

"Why?" I asked, sarcastically, as if I didn't know she had just been in a screaming match with Yuma.

"Yuma ALWAYS defends him! Why does she always side with him?! He doesn't do anything good for her or this family and yet we still need to respect him."

"Well, he is our father, as much as we hate to admit it; we have to respect him to his face, at least."

"I'm not fake like that; I don't like him, and he knows I don't, so why do I have to pretend to like someone who knows I don't like him? He's so disgusting."

I sighed, "I don't know Ilham, I really don't want to talk about this right now, it's early."

"It's because you kiss Yuma's ass; of course, you aren't going to agree with me."

"Ughhh," I moaned again. "No it's not, aren't you tired of all this drama? It's too much of a headache."

"It's too much of a headache," she mimicked in a mocking tone. I rolled my eyes as my phone alerted me that I'd received a text. Grateful, I hurriedly looked to the screen and saw that Mr. Evenson had texted me.

"Hello, my daughter, how are you?" it read.

I smiled slightly as I responded, "save me pleeeeeassseee I cannot be home right now :(." Clicking send, I tried to drone out the angry insults Ilham was going off on a tangent with. She seemed to get angrier and angrier as the days went by and I honestly didn't blame her; living under this roof was getting stressful and I was surprised we all hadn't completely lost our heads yet.

My phone buzzed again, "Haha sure thing, how about Barnes and Noble?"

I smiled wide then and texted back, "YES PLEASE!"

Clicking send, I jumped out of bed and began my routine of getting ready. Ilham watched from the corner of her eye and commented on my excitement to meet up with Mr. Evenson.

"That's gross, he's a perv; he's like 60 years old and he's hanging out with you."

"You're gross for thinking like that, you're the only one who thinks that so keep your opinions to yourself. He's a better father than Alzalim is."

I was seriously annoyed now. Mr. Evenson is my art teacher; ever since we transferred back into a city school, he was always there to consult with me and guide me through the drama of our family. He was always willing to lend a hand and listen to my problems. Mr. Everson was the best adopted father anyone could ask for and I was very lucky to have him-- there was no way I'd allow anyone to disrespect him that way.

She continued with her string of strong opinions that she stuck to, proudly, about him; but I continued to pay no mind to her. She was an angry person and angry people love misery as their company. Fifteen *minutes later, Mr. Evenson was outside, honking his horn as I kissed Yuma goodbye and jumped into the backseat of his car.*

"Thank you so much for saving me! I could not be in that house as they continued arguing--too much for one weekend."

He laughed, "I can imagine; I bet Ilham is blowing steam from her ears at the moment."

"Spot on," I confirmed annoyed. I had informed him of the recent events that were occurring with Ilham and Yuma, as of late. The both of them had been arguing daily now and it had become unbearable. Their arguments would last all day or would be triggered by the smallest things--the rest of us felt stifled in this atmosphere.

"Well it's a good thing we'll be at Barnes and Noble--get away from the war that's still going on strong within your life."

"No kidding, I'm glad to get out of there."

"Now from my understanding, your father isn't home right?" he asked trying to get a grasp of the events that have been happening.

"No, he's been gone for about a year now; we don't know when he's coming back nor do I care. I hope that he actually ran away from home; it'd be the best magic trick to ever occur."

He laughed then, "That would be a good trick indeed, don't worry sweetie, you'll get out of there in no time. You'll be in college and working for your future."

"Yea, but I feel like that time will come, but nothing will change. I'll still be trapped in this tug of war with my parents."

"Well, that's what you haven't experienced yet; in college it's all about self-discovery. You'll learn what works best for Amani and what Amani will accept in her life--and what she won't."

"It's not that easy is it?" I asked as we pulled into the parking lot.

While he parked the car, I grabbed my phone on the seat and hopped out to hurry into the building with the smell of new books that made my heart content. This store filled with books and coffee was my sanctuary and didn't he know it.

With a big smile on my face, I ran into the nearest aisle and scanned all the books to find anything that would catch my eye. It was during times like these that I was able to forget about everything going on--I was able to escape for just a few hours--but I relished those moments and held them close to my heart, during times when I just wanted to cry.

"It is that easy; it's your life Amani. Live it the way you want to. It's just that easy."

I shook my head with a slight frown across my face. Turning to face him, I saw how strong the hope was in his face. He was hopeful of the future I had, but I don't think he knew just how hard it was actually going to be for me.

"No, it's not that easy Mr. Evenson. What many people, who are not in this predicament, don't understand is that there's this invisible responsibility bred into us. We don't simply think that it's our life and choose to live it, however we please. It just doesn't work like that; we carry this overwhelming responsibility--it's always present--it's always in the back of our minds, hovering over the things we say, the people we hang out with, and engrained within the stitches of our DNA. It is who we are. We are a legacy--a printed copy of the lineage we are supposed to carry on and the heritage we are supposed to pass on without fail. We don't just simply leave all that to live the life we want; this is bigger than myself. It affects our honor, our pride, our reputation, protects our history and what we make of our future. I am not the one who holds the reigns of my life, per say. I may carry one side of it, but the other is led by them--they influence every part of every decision I make. If I just got up and left, I wouldn't want to throw others in the flame, due to my actions."

My point seemed to dawn on him then and the hope vanished from his face, as he stood there letting my words sink in. I knew it was a hard *thing to understand, but given the tone I was speaking to him with, my situation was a lot more precarious than he originally thought. It made me realize something then; it would be hard for others to understand what we, as a family unit, were going through because to the general public it was easy to just do what they wanted to. Explaining that internal struggle to someone who doesn't have the same tribulations, was hard. It's not easy to put into words what we go through--that we simply can't escape. The entire experience is hard to put into words..children in our culture carry an immense amount of pressure and some of us crack under the weight of it all. Others break entirely and run off or do something rebellious just to be set free from the expectations set upon us. Our parents don't realize the weight they continue to pile on us; and if they do they don't care. I just hope I was able to shed a small light on what it is that I've been going through, than he previously understood.*

"I see what you mean now, I see the imperceptible chains that you and the women in your situation have been wearing and it's sad that you guys are going through such hard times. No one should ever be forced into that or made to feel that they have no choice in the matter."

"Yea," I agreed, as I watched a child struggle to get a book off a shelf, until her mother grabbed her hand and started to pull her away. The young girl tried pushing back her mother for a second, before giving up. When it was all said and done, the girl just stared at the book she yearned to reach, with nothing but a frown.

I could feel the sadness of the child and knew what it felt like to want one thing but be pushed in another direction. It was hard, truly hard, but it was the life I was meant to deal with for the moment; I could do nothing but hope and pray for something better.

"Let's get a cup of coffee," he recommended. I nodded my head and allowed him to lead us to the Starbucks stationed within the store. Standing in line, I contemplated the words we exchanged as the sound of

grinding coffee beans and the smell of heaven floated to my nose. I began to wonder if I'd ever find the courage to do what I wanted for myself or if I'd forever remain in the shadow of my people. Was it that easy to leave? Was it so simple to just get up and go? Surely something terrible would happen if I chose this path. But that wasn't something I'd be able to find out unless I actually did it. And right now, I had no urgency to do so; I didn't want to risk anything right now, considering I am new to this 'against the grain' kind of action. Sitting at our table by the window with a cup of coffee nuzzled against the palms of my hands, I took a moment to breathe in the delectable smell. There was something about its intoxicating scent that made me numb to everything else, something that made life just a tad bit better.

I scanned the crowd then and saw the different emotions running through people's faces, as they continued their conversations. I wondered if anyone was going through anything similar, wondering if they too put on a face for the rest of the world, so that no one would ask questions. And if so, did they feel guilty like me? For a moment I thought about others who are going through worse--people who are dealing with no water and no food, the loss of life, the loss of resources they needed to survive. Did I have the right to complain? No. But I had the ability to write it out; how would that work I wondered?, Should I just write about the events Yuma went through from my perspective? Could I explain the years leading up to this moment? Would it even help anyone?

I didn't know. But I would write anyway.

CHAPTER 25

Summertime News

"The most beautiful people we have known are those who
have known defeat, known suffering, known struggle,
known loss and have found their way out of those depths."

– Elisabeth Kubler-Ross

O ften times we know when something great is going to happen. We sense it--it's coming. The feeling of waking up with it in your bones was thrilling--knowing that whatever the day had, it was going to end off great. You feel energized, excited, and ready to push on with the day because, whatever that opportunity was, it was out there for you, waiting for you to grab it. It made you tingle with an alertness that was unmatched. That's what I woke up to--the feeling that something great was on its way. And I was ready for it; I was more than deserving of it--it had been a long time coming and I was more than ready for it to finally arrive.

The buzzing of my phone caught my attention with the sound loud against the counter at which I was sitting. It was early; the morning dew left last night's rain scented in the air. With the crunch of cereal filling my mind, I was zoned out thinking about, nothing new.

"Hello?" I answered,

"Hello?" Yuma answered back, "Amani I'm going to pick you up in 15 minutes, be ready."

"Okay," I responded without question. Whatever she wanted to see me for must have been important if she didn't wait for a confirmation before hanging up the phone. But my heart was not racing in fear, so my instincts were telling me that I wasn't in trouble. Curious, I made sure to get dressed in a manner that Yuma would approve of. But knowing Yuma, fifteen minutes meant that she would be here in thirty. So, I sat down on the roof that attached to the outside of my window; it was a beautiful day with the slight chill on your skin, but it felt nice. It was one of those days where it was calm and still, the streets weren't too loud, but it also wasn't too silent. Cars drove by, here and there, filling the atmosphere with vibration.

My mind wandered then, wondering what my life would be like a year from now, where I would be and how successful I would end up. I always woke up with a feeling that I was meant for greater things. I don't know why I was so sure that it was bound to happen for me, but I just knew, ya know? I was scared, naturally, the way everyone was. I was a child in school for so long, but now I would soon be thrown into the world, with no free time, and chained to a nine to five job that I possibly wouldn't like. But it was a story I was down to write.

My phone buzzed, alerting me of a text: *From Khaleel: how does painting sound as our first date? :P*

I smiled, excited for this new chapter of my life. Clicking 'respond,' I quickly typed back: *To Khaleel: sounds great, let's see what skills you have with a paint brush :P*

The sound of a car honking made my reflexes kick in; turning quickly, I noticed Yuma pulling up and ready to pick me up. Shoving my phone away, I was in complete surprise that she got there so quickly and on time. Jumping back into my room, I hurriedly made my way down the stairs and outside. My phone started ringing, without looking I knew it was going to be Yuma calling to tell me to rush myself without noticing that I was already beside the passenger door. Knocking on the window, she looked up to see me standing there and unlocked the door to let me in.

"*Salam wa alaikum Yuma,*" I greeted her. Clicking my seat belt into place, I looked at her and kissed her cheek. It seemed that each time I saw her she grew prettier and prettier. If I aged the way she did I would be completely fine with aging--she blossomed into such a beautiful woman and, God, was I happy that I came out looking like her.

"*Wa alaikum salam,*" she responded. Turning the car into drive, she pushed forward and headed deeper into the parts of the street that were more secluded and private before parking. I was confused, we weren't anywhere in particular, so I assumed she just wanted to speak. The fact that this wasn't done over the phone is what made me curious, as to the topic of the conversation.

"Yuma is everything okay?" I asked nervous. She looked at me. I tried searching for any sign that would give away whatever she wanted to talk about, but I couldn't find anything. I began to worry then. She shuffled in the back before pulling out a large white envelope to the front of the car. Setting it on my lap she told me to look in it and read what I pulled out from it. I swallowed then, trying to moisten my mouth that was suddenly dry. Taking the semi heavy envelope, I opened it. Sliding the papers out, I turned them over and read the top section:

Confirmation of Divorce.

I stopped breathing for a second as I let the words sink in; there was no way she had the courage to finally divorce Alzalim, after twenty-one years of verbal and physical abuse from him and his family. There was no way she figured out how to break the chains that had held her captive for so many years. Coming from the woman who preached to me that I must first and always present myself as a Palestinian woman before an American woman, I was shocked. Typically, women in my culture never divorced, even if they were being cheated on or abused. Even though our religion made such a marriage forbidden, women in our culture were afraid to divorce. They were afraid of the rumors and whispers being spread about them, afraid that others would think they divorced because they wanted to have sex with other men or that they were already seeing another man on the side. No one ever blamed the ex-husband and never mentioned that he cheated or abused his wife. And if they knew, they paid little to no mind to it; so long as it was done by the hands or through the actions of a man, it was acceptable.

Yet here it was: Confirmation of the divorce that was long overdue. The fact that she stood on her own two feet and decided to go through this process, alone, was admirable. She finally realized her sense of self-worth and left him. She knew that there was more to her than a man and realized that she could offer herself more than her pathetic, disgrace of a husband could. She knew she had to move forward in her life, as a single mother, to achieve the dreams she wanted to achieve. I recalled a strong memory then--a moment when she'd been helpless and learned more than anything, that day, that she had to rely on herself and not him-- that in order for our family to foster and grow, she had to be the one to carry us. Not him.

It was a year after his release from prison; things seemed to be in the swing of normalcy and our empty apartment finally became a furnished one. Having Alzalim around started to feel natural, as if he had never been gone. We'd all joke around with him during the daylight hours in which he was awake, because he worked all night at a paper production factory. Usually, when he came home, he'd go straight to bed from the exhaustion. We missed him a lot during those times because we rarely ever got to see him and when he did have free time, he invested it all into a cell phone store he was trying to create a block away from our house. He believed that if he were to get the store started close by, he'd be able to quit his job and get more free time with us. Yuma supported him in his venture; she became his advisor in a way, but warned him that he should check to see, first, if the particular cell phone company would approve of the location before we, as a family, invested so much money in such a project. But he assured her that he knew what he was doing and that it was a great location.

Five months later, once production was almost done, nearly all cell phone companies denied the location and, thus, we were stranded with no cell phone store and thousands wasted down the drain. Yuma was livid, yelling and screaming at him, reminding him that she had told him to check and see if the location was confirmed first. What made matters worse was that that same day she found out he opened two credit cards under her name and had charged over five thousand dollars on it. She nearly had a heart attack once she came across that discovery--her fear over what to do, to pay it without a job, consumed her. She was a stay at home mom, at the time, and seeing those numbers caused her to panic.

She called Siti and told her about the events that happened, asking for help and asking her to set her son in line before our family suffered more than we already had. She begged her to get him straightened out because he was being a child, upset that he didn't have the free time he was accustomed to in prison and trying to find any loophole to not have to work anymore. But the worst had yet to come and once it arrived, it left us speechless.

One hot evening, Siti arrived at our house with Alzalim. We all gathered at our apartment window and watched as Siti got out of the car.

Ilham opened the window as quickly as she could, shouting, "Hi Siti," with as much excitement that I lacked at the sight of her. Siti looked up to us and smiled before waving back at Ilham who held baby Nur firmly in her arms. Since Nur's birth she was kept strictly near Ilham's side as if she had been the one to have birthed her. Always up and ready to cater to our baby sister, Ilham became more of a mother to her than Yuma was. It surprised me, given that we were both in the 8th grade and yet, she seemed so mature to be able to care for another life the way she did. I could see the love that consumed her in the way she stared at Nur; the awe that couldn't be wiped clean.

Entering our apartment, Siti sat down once we all greeted her. She looked like she carried a lot on her shoulders with the amount of stress visible on her face. I had a feeling she was not bringing us good news during this visit.

Before she even sat down, Yuma was already in tears and begging Siti to fix the situation Alzalim had put her in. Siti sat down on the couch, while Yuma dropped to her knees beside her, cupping Siti's hands within hers.

"Please, you have to fix this; he opened two credit cards in my name and charged over five thousand dollars on them! I don't have a job, what am I supposed to do?"

Siti's face shifted from frustration to anger. Turning her attention towards Alzalim, she began yelling, "Now why would you go and do something as stupid as that?! You don't think! You never think before you do anything!"

Alzalim grew annoyed then, "I needed it for the store! How am I supposed to get a credit card with my credit! I was going to pay it back once the store was up and running but it didn't get approved!"

Yuma was now looking at him with the purest look of disgust I've ever seen on her face, "I swear I don't understand how anyone can be as dumb as you."

Siti sighed then, "This just makes everything that much more complicated, because the reason I came here today is to let you know that the house has been sold."

Yuma looked from Alzalim to Siti as the news settled in. "What do you mean, the downstairs is rented out?" she asked for clarification. In the house we lived in there were two apartments to which Yuma was referring to.

"No, the entire house has been sold; you have two weeks to sell whatever you have to sell and move elsewhere."

Yuma's mouth dropped as Ilham and myself sat there, confused as to exactly what was going on. I knew there was a lot of tension, but I didn't understand why Yuma was so angry at the time. Siti continued speaking then, mentioning that they (she and Alzalim) had bought a bar with the sales profit of our home.

Yuma's face screamed before her voice could catch up, "What?! A bar?! You're selling our home to purchase a bar?! No! No! I'm not letting that happen, I gave you my last bit of gold to pay you for this house!! You have no right!"

What I didn't know then, at that age, was the deal made between my parents. One of Yuma's biggest dreams was owning a house of her own so that she'd one day be stress free, without a care, or any threat of her children being without a roof over their heads. Siti had bought our house with the intention to sell it to my mother, who in turn, would give her the gold from her wedding.

Palestinian weddings are traditionally very long events that can be up to a week or two, with parties every night filled with close family, friends, and extended family. Once the celebration is over, the bride's family begins another ceremony to say their goodbyes to their daughter, out of respect to the new chapter of her life. During this ceremony the gold bought by her fiancé and his family is then placed upon her in front of the audience, her beauty being showcased for everyone to celebrate. Yuma's gold became more and more valuable over the years, something she knew even when she first became married, so she kept it safely hidden away until her dream called for the gold to be removed from its safe place and handed over to Siti.

It hurts me now to think about such a cruel act. I couldn't imagine my dream being ripped from me in the manner it had been with Yuma.

Siti's face frowned in anger then, "I do have the right; it's under my name is it not? I bought the house, so I can do whatever I want with it. You should be lucky I never kicked you guys out!"

My heart painfully beat then; I didn't know then much of what was happening, but whenever I saw Yuma in pain I was in pain. To see her so upset and broken, on the floor, made me so angry and yet I was powerless in this circumstance.

"No! How dare you! How dare you try and sell this house for a bar! Think of your grandkids--where would they live?!"

"On top of the bar of course," Alzalim chimed in then, his smug face content in the decision he and his mom had made. "There's an apartment atop the bar; the family can live there."

Yuma's bewildered eyes moved from Siti to Alzalim then: "You expect my kids to live in a house full of sin? To live where the Shatan (devil) operates most? In a house where you'll be making profit out of haram (forbidden) drinks? No! You are not doing this to our family! Not after you put me in debt--you owe us!"

Alzalim shrugged his shoulders then. "You either live there or in the streets; it's your choice. Take the kids with you," he responded, throwing us away. I wanted to spit on him then, with his comments only making me angrier the more I looked at him. He was a disgusting, vile man to put Yuma in such a state. My heart went out to her, seeing her with her face white and bewildered and her eyes wide and scared. You could tell she couldn't believe what was going on--none of us did. How can two people really just sell a house right under our noses and think it's okay for a practicing Muslim family to live inside a building with a bar operating downstairs? It made no sense--no sense at all. On top of everything they were throwing at her, she was given two weeks to figure out how she was going to sell everything, as well as find a place to live.

"How..." she gasped breathless, "How did this happen? You guys walk in showing your true form: Shatan. Both of you are Shatan. My kids, where will my kids live?" she rocked back and forth in disbelief. Tears streamed down her face, her body shaking with regret and fear. I cried then, too, as I rushed to her; this wasn't fair--this wasn't fair at all. She didn't deserve everything that was happening. Was this how he repaid her for her loyalty to him? This is how they treated a woman whose undying dedication had pulled Alzalim through those years in prison. I was angry, crying, and I didn't know what to do.

"I suggest you start a house sale to get some money in your pockets, if you aren't living at the bar," was all Siti said before making her exit. I had a deep frown on my face with such malice behind it and I wanted to go postal. This was unfair, completely unfair to Yuma. She had paid out of her pocket to get this apartment for us and they screwed her over. It was frustrating to be so young that you couldn't help in any way. I felt like I was just being chained and forced to watch her suffer such arduous tasks. Why was she being put through so much in such a short time? I hurt for her, deeply.

I remember at the end of the night--when everything calmed down for the time being--she approached all four of us. We had been silent the rest of the day, knowing that Yuma was trying to figure out what her next *steps would be. She was thrown into this predicament with such short notice and had no time to prepare. Her eyes were heavy and bloodshot with exhaustion causing her lids to become inflamed.*

"We'll get through this, I promise. Allah puts his strongest warriors in the toughest of battles, even when they believe they cannot overcome them."

"But why?" I whispered.

"Because Amani, he's showing us that what we believe to be the most we can handle, only turns out to be the starting point of what we can really do. Don't lose faith in yourself or in me. We will have to learn to stand up on our own; relying on others has only come to make us bow down to those who oppress us."

Those two weeks we had left were busy; it required the entire family unit to come together and get things sorted out. Alzalim didn't dare show his face during the rest of our time there and Yuma barely ate. I was afraid, but I didn't show it, because Ilham didn't show it. We had to be strong for Yuma, because only she was allowed to cry; we didn't want to add to her pain.

Upon her return one evening, she held a pile of massive white posters and markers. Ilham and I looked at her and then at one another confused. She sat down cross legged then and called Ayman over from his room. The pitter patter of feet was heard before he plopped down right beside us.

"Now, I need you guys to do me a big favor: Ilham and Amani are going to write, 'Moving Sale! Everything Must Go!' on the posters and Ayman, you're going to hang it up with this staple gun. Be careful though; don't put your finger underneath."

Nodding our heads, we took the task very seriously as we diligently worked through the day. It was hard work for us all, given that tasks were being thrown left and right. Ilham took charge of pricing, as I placed the sticker on each item. I caught the sight of Yuma smiling a bit, as we struggled to place a sticker on a piece of furniture. I also detected the sadness behind the smile and knew that she was keeping a tough front now, in order to motivate us. I couldn't fully comprehend then, as a child, the burden of raising four kids, the stress involved with paying bills and keeping us healthy and fed. Yuma made it seem so easy at times, even when we had no furniture--no table to place our home cooked meals. She made everything home, no matter where we were or what situation we happened to find ourselves in.

There was also, once, a time when she turned a negative situation into a bonding moment for us as a family. Long ago, after our parents had been fighting for God knows how long, Ayman, Ilham and I felt nervous to leave our rooms. The atmosphere was thick with tension and it didn't seem like the right time to leave the safety of the walls we were occupying. A half hour later, a delicious scent wafted through the cracks of the doors, causing Ayman to pause the Nintendo 64 he was in the process of playing,

"You guys smell that?" he asked us curiously. Ilham and I put down our toys and sniffed the air.

"Yea, that smells good," we confirmed. Like the curious kids we were, we jumped up and stepped out of the room. As we turned the corner into the living room, we watched as Yuma set up a big, fluffy blanket on the floor before setting down plates and utensils on top of it. It was a sight unlike any I've seen before: A warm and inviting aura surrounded the living room. She sat down in front of one of the plates and motioned for us to join her. We all took our seats beside one another and finished waiting for Yuma to put the food on our plates. I watched her then: calm, collected and beautiful, you couldn't even tell she had just been in a dispute with Alzalim just before this moment. Her aging beauty was so calm against the backdrop of her dark hair--she was a sight to see and, in her arms, I felt safe and brave. I felt I could conquer the world. She didn't allow the

unsettling argument to stop her from joining us for dinner and a rerun of Pokémon. For the first time during that period, she actually sat with us and took her time to eat and enjoy the meal with us.

In motherhood, there was sacrifice more often than one would believe. Mothers tend to put aside their feelings and desires to ensure the wellbeing and survival of their children. I never noticed the warrior within her then and never noticed that she was, in fact, the sole reason we are alive and well today, because she had made it her life's mission to set aside her dreams, in order, for us to reach ours. She wouldn't put selfish desires above our needs and she would never let her stress push her to abandon us.

Courage takes many forms. It takes a strong will to do what's right for the better good. Many times, the courage a mother undertakes is overlooked or simply excused as the "duties" of a mother and it's not seen for what it really is. Behind each adult lies a parent who's guided them; on average, they're mostly single mothers taking up the responsibility of raising acceptable members of society. We pay no mind to the mental stress and burdens put on them, because it's expected of mothers to raise the children. But when you sit back to reflect on it, they are the reason we remain true and unique to ourselves and to our values today. It takes a certain level of strength and a massive amount of courage to take on the blank slate of a child and raise them to uphold the set standards and morals of society, by yourself. Such tasks are daunting and yet, a mother's instinct accomplishes all of this, quite effortlessly.

Sitting in her car today, I saw it all clearly now. The wind danced with the trees beside us--the sound of them swaying against the wind created a chorus of applause on behalf of Yuma. The sun crept out from behind its clouded gaze and light poured through our windows. The atmosphere felt different then; holding the papers in my hand, I turned to get a good look at her and saw someone marvelous. A woman who was worthy of praise. A woman who, through every challenge, never let a single tribulation crush her. She was a hero, she had broken free of such a torturous marriage. As it stood now, she knew what would become of her with the divorce confirmation, she knew what to expect from all those who would hear of it, and yet, I teared up at the sight of something I hadn't seen in over three years. As wide as the ocean and as white as a pearl, it shined ever so beautifully against the sunlight. I was so mesmerized by it that I wouldn't let myself blink--in fear of losing sight of it. It was a sign of hope; something our family had needed for so long... something I had needed to see for so long...Yuma was smiling.

RANINE is an up and coming author whose talent in stitching words together will leave you entangled in her web. Ever since she first picked up a pencil all she dreamed about was writing novels, finishing her first draft in the 6th grade she knew early on what her passion in life was. Ranine dreams of writing for a living and one day raising a family of book lovers of her own. You can always find her with coffee in one hand and writing with the other.

She is the child of Palestinian immigrants. Her mother immigrated from Jerusalem to America, and Yuma's Smile is her own attempt to make sense of the collision of cultures she saw growing up. Born and raised in the States, Ranine grew up blending these cultures and struggled to find the balance between the two. Ranine holds a B.A in human science and family development from Syracuse University and is currently studying for her Master's in marketing communications.